Tails from the Front Lines 2:

The Thin Blue Line

Edited by
Carol Hightshoe

WolfSinger Publications ⟨ Security, Colorado

Acknowledgements

Dog Days – © 2011 Jonathan Maberry Productions
Originally Published as an audio original by Blackstone Audio
They're Smuggling What? – © 2023 by Dana Bell
Horn – © 2023 by DJ Tyrer
The Roxy Ruling – © 2017 by Lisa Timpf
Originally Published in *New Myths*, Issue 40, September 15, 2017,
under the title "Roxy's Rule"
Teamwork – © 2023 by Bailey Finn
The K9 of Spellstruck Academy – © 2023 by Kendra Petresky
Where the Hearth Is – © 2021 by Lisa Timpf
Originally Published in *Home for the Howlidays*,
edited by M.L.D. Curelas, published by Tyche Books Ltd., 2021
Mick and Me – © 2023 by Jean Martin
K9 Jinx – © 2023 by Deputy Nicholas Witherite

For permission requests, please contact WolfSinger Publications at:
editor@wolfsingerpubs.com

Cover Photo – K9 Jinx
Provided by the El Paso County Sheriff's Office

ISBN 978-1-944637-33-0

Printed and bound in the United States of America

Table of Contents

Dog Days

Jonathan Maberry

~1~

When you do what I do, you know Death. You understand him, and his consorts, pain and loss.

These things are no longer abstractions. They aren't rarities that intrude into your routine, like when Uncle Bob cashes it in at Sunny Acres on his ninety-third birthday, or when one of your drinking buddies strokes out on the eighth hole, two under par but all the wrong clubs in his bag.

No, when your job is war, when you are a killer, Death is a more frequent co-pilot than God.

Death is around you, he's in you, he's *of* you. Sometimes he's your friend, the best friend you'll ever have—when you're down to the last bullet in your mag and you squeeze the trigger while running and he punches the bad guy's ticket in what you'll always believe was an impossible shot. Not impossible; it's just that death was your wingman that day. Tomorrow he might be going to war under a totally different flag. Death's like that. He's not fickle; he wants every-one on his side.

Every warrior has the same connection. Maybe there are gods and angels up there screwing with the fates of men and Death is the great cosmic bouncer. Maybe there are gods of war and Death is their angel. Maybe Death is more selective than we know, but if so, he has an agenda we'll never understand. I know I don't. I've killed bad men, but bad men have killed better men than me.

Who knows why Death favors one man over another on any given day? A lot of guys believe that Death—or someone—listens to prayers and follows rules. These guys wear talismans into battle. Crosses and *hamsa* hands, lucky socks and tattoos of saints drilled into their skin. Sometimes it helps. Sometimes that's the only way we can identify the dead.

Every warrior strives to understand Death. They love him and they hate him in the same breath. In every breath. They try to know him, to know his mind.

Me?

Yeah, I know Death. But I don't worship him and I don't fear him.

He wants me, he can have me.

For me, it's a jealousy thing. I envy the cold bastard.

Because he took her.

Her.

My love. Death took the only grace I had left in life.

Death took her and he owns her. She's with him, down in that cold, dark palace in the dirt.

And it hurts so bad.

If I thought that a bullet—from my own gun or one I walked in front of—could buy my passage across the River Styx to her side, if I thought that, I'd ride the bullet all the way down.

But it doesn't work like that.

The priests and the shrinks and your friends all tell you that it doesn't work that way.

Death, you see, is also a jealous son of a bitch. He doesn't share.

So—I keep living.

And I envy Death for the grace he has and the Grace I lost.

~2~

They buried her in September.

By the end of that month, I was able to walk without a cane. My hair was growing back, the double vision was gone.

The shakes? Still had those. Nausea, acid stomach? Yeah.

"When was the last time you had a good night's sleep?" asked Rudy Sanchez. Friend, shrink, drinking buddy, fellow mourner. He loved Grace too. Not in the same way. She was family to him. She was that and more to me. Every single day we can both see the hole in the world where she should be.

"Cowboy?" he prompted.

I shrugged. We were sitting on beach chairs in my dad's back-yard. Beers and illegal Cubans. Couple of steaks on a slow grill. Spanish music on the boombox.

"Out loud," said Rudy. "In words."

"I don't know, man. I catch a few hours."

"In a row?"

I shot him the finger which shut him up long enough for me to finish my beer. He turned the steaks while I got us fresh bottles. Yuengling for me, Anchor Steam for him. He accepted his bottle even though he wasn't finished with the one resting on his stomach, and he arched an eyebrow over the opaque lenses of his sunglasses as I twisted the cap off of mine.

"How many is that?"

"Somewhere between not enough and fuck you," I said.

He sighed.

The afternoon was burning its way toward twilight. It was weirdly hot for the first of October. The fourth straight day in the nineties, with humidity to match. If someone left the back door of Hell open it would be like this. We smoked our cigars and drank our beer and gazed with thousand-yard stares on the wreckage of our lives.

Well, of my life.

After a while I said, "I went in yesterday."

"To the Warehouse?"

"Yeah. I was hoping Church would be there. I wanted to tell him—you know—face to face."

I could feel Rudy studying me but I didn't look at him.

"Tell him what?" he asked.

"That I was done."

"You've been saying that since Grace died, Joe."

"It's true."

He tapped some ash onto the grass that curled around his flip-flops. "I know. You said that you can't do this anymore, that you were ruined. That's the word you used. 'Ruined.'"

I said nothing.

"But you're healing," he said. "The doctors said that you would make a complete recovery—and before you jump all over me *again*, we both know that they were only talking about a physical recovery. They understand that emotional and psychological recovery will take longer."

"'Take longer'?" I echoed, loading it with the scorn it deserved.

"Yes, Joe. I know you think that this is something you won't or can't get past, but you will. Am I saying that you'll heal completely and without scar tissue? No, and you know that I don't think that.

At the same time, you should try to address the fact that you seem to feel that you healing is somehow an insult to Grace's memory. That it's a disservice to her sacrifice."

"It is."

"It isn't," he insisted, his tone shifting from best friend to therapist in the way it does when he believes he's right. He usually is right, but this time I couldn't see how.

I sipped more beer and watched the last lonely fireflies burn themselves out above the line of carefully tended hedges. It was a quiet neighborhood. Before Rudy and I joined the Department of Military Sciences back in June, I really liked the quiet order of this place; but now it felt like it belonged to a different world. A better world than mine, no doubt, but definitely not where I belonged. For months now my life had been about weird science, doomsday plots, terrorism, gunplay, and death. While I'd been fighting the good fight, I never noticed that with every battle I fought, every life I took, I was being slowly evicted from the world I knew. Sure, I could come here and drink beer and even smoke a Cuban, but it was window dressing. It was play-acting someone who I wasn't ever going to be again.

Rudy knew it too.

He'd warned me about it from the start. When Mr. Church had first hijacked me into the DMS, Rudy had warned me about the mark on the soul that violence always left. I hadn't listened closely enough, hadn't heard the full lesson. I'd thought he meant that whenever *I* used violence it would mark me; but that wasn't the whole picture. Any violence around me, any violence I cared about, was going to gouge its gang sign into me too.

I cared about Grace, first as a friend, then as a lover.

And now I was so badly marked, so thoroughly mauled by everything that had happened, that I knew that I had become a stranger to the people who knew me. It was easiest for my dad to pretend he didn't see it. He was running for mayor and he had the campaign to keep him busy. My brother was still a detective, and when he looked at me, I could see the natural cop wariness kick in at high gear. He knew I was different. He saw the bruises on my body, the pink surgical lines, and the bitter grief that I could not hide, and without ever saying so in words he told me to keep my horrors away from his family.

Did I blame him?

No way.

"Are you listening to anything I'm saying?" asked Rudy, and I realized that he had been talking for a couple of minutes and I hadn't heard a word.

"No," I said.

"Well, at least you didn't sugarcoat that with a lie." He turned to face me. "Anyway, I asked what happened when you went to the Warehouse yesterday."

"The plan was to pack. I wanted to get my shit out of there and maybe see about resubmitting my application to the FBI."

"Wouldn't that be a big step down? I'm not talking about pay and benefits, but in utilizing your potential as a—"

"Screw that."

"After the DMS, the FBI is likely to be less of a challenge."

"Fine by me."

"Even boring."

"Boring sounds good."

"No," he said, "it doesn't. You think it does because you're still traumatized, but let's be adults here, Joe—you'd never be able to work in something that mundane again."

"The FBI is hardly mundane, Rude. Geez, they're part of Homeland and—"

"—And they don't do what we do. What you do."

I didn't reply to that. Instead I said, "When I got to the Warehouse, Church was out. He's up in Brooklyn. But he left some stuff for me in my quarters. Two things. Two options. Against one wall was a stack of empty boxes so I could pack up my shit and leave."

"And the other thing?"

"There was a file folder on the bed. An intelligence folder. Inside was a surveillance photo of a tall man taken two days ago at the *Riviera Dei Fiori*, on the Italian Riviera."

"Oh? Who was the man in the photo?"

I drew on the cigar until the coal glowed hot and orange. "Conrad Veder," I said.

Rudy gaped and spilled his beer down the front of his shirt.

"*Dios mio!*" he said, and uttered a string of low, vicious curses in gutter Spanish.

"Yeah," I said.

Conrad Veder.

The man who had murdered Grace.

~3~

Later, when the sky was littered with stars and the cooler was filled with empties and melted ice, Rudy and I still sat in the beach chairs. We hadn't spoken in nearly an hour.

Finally, Rudy said, "You're going after him."

A statement, not a question.

I nodded.

"When?"

"I don't know. Soon. I talked to our guys in Italy, the ones who obtained the surveillance photos, and Veder dropped off the radar again. Everyone's looking for him and as soon as he's spotted, they'll get word to me right away."

"Don't bite my head off when I ask this, but what shape are you in to go after that man?"

I shrugged.

"Joe, Veder is one of the most highly skilled and dangerous assassins in the world. Even Mr. Church said that he was in a class by himself. A master of every kind of firearm, skilled in unarmed combat…"

"I don't intend to challenge him to a duel, Rudy. I'm going to find him and kill him."

Under most other circumstances Rudy would rise to the challenge in that kind of statement and we'd wrangle about murder versus self-defense, but not lately. He would never come out and say so, but he wanted Veder dead too.

"Are you taking the team? Top and Bunny would—"

"No. This is mine."

"Is that wise?"

"I don't care. This is going to be a hunt and it may take a long time. I can't drag around a whole team when I'm sniffing out a trail."

"So—is that why Mr. Church has been talking about your dog?"

"Dog? I don't have a dog."

"Mr. Church told me a couple of days ago you were going to

be training a military dog. Are you doing that to help you hunt this man?"

"Rudy, I don't have a dog and I'm not planning on getting one. You must have misunderstood what Church was saying."

But, as it turns out, I was the one who was wrong.

I did get a dog.

~4~

"I don't want a dog," I said.

We were in the big training room at the Warehouse. The trainer looked from Rudy to Church. "I—"

"You could use a companion," suggested Rudy.

"You need a partner," advised Church.

"I don't want a god damned—"

"You have a choice," Church cut in. "You train with the dog and take him with you when we get a fresh lead on Veder, or you don't train with him and I turn the lead over to Interpol and you can read about it in the paper."

I started to tell him what he could do with that idea, but he interrupted me again.

"I'm sorry, Captain, for giving you the misapprehension that this was a debate. Enjoy your training." With that he turned away. Over his shoulder he said, "Bonding is an important part of the training process. I'll leave you to it."

"Hey!" I yelled, but Church was already talking on his cell phone. Or pretending to.

The trainer, Zan Rosin, smiled hopefully up at me. "He's a very nice dog," she said. "He's exceptionally smart and has already passed through standard and advanced training in search and rescue, bomb detection, bark and hold, high-speed disarm, cover and conceal-ment..." Her words trickled down and stopped when she saw my expression.

I glowered down at her prodigy of a dog. A white Shepherd. Two hundred and five pounds, with brown eyes that were currently sizing me up the way Rudy sizes up a porterhouse steak.

"He's very friendly," she said.

The dog bared his teeth.

"Look," said Rudy, "he's smiling at you."

The dog began to growl.

"Or not," Rudy amended. "Call me later, Cowboy." He did not actually run, but he walked away very fast.

The trainer and I watched him go, and then she looked up at me with a trembling smile. "His name is Ghost," she said.

I gave her a withering stare. "I'm a cat person. I don't even like dogs."

Ghost continued to growl. Neither of us was trying to hide our true feelings.

~5~

Conrad Veder dropped off the face of the earth. Interpol and the CIA were looking for him. Church had every resource the DMS could spare looking for him. Barrier, the British counterpart of the DMS, was looking for him. Nobody was able to find him.

I knew that Church wanted to get me back into the fold, to have me take over command of the Warehouse and resume my position as leader of Echo Team. But that wasn't what I wanted.

The only thing Church got was me partnering with the dog.

It was no walk in the park though. Not for me, and not for the dog. I'm pretty sure the handler, Zan Rosin, began drinking her lunch by the end of the first week.

Training with Ghost was a weird experience for me. I really am a cat person. I have a middle-aged marmalade tabby name Cobbler who disliked dogs as much as I did. When I brought Ghost home for the first time, Cobbler and he failed to bond in a spectacular fashion. Furniture and crockery were destroyed. Neighbors almost called the cops.

Eventually they staked out which sections of my apartment belonged to each of them, and yes, pissing on territorial lines was involved, damn it.

In training sessions, however, Ghost and I began to find a rhythm. Zan wasn't joking when she said Ghost had been highly trained already. He was top of his class every time, which is why Church acquired him for me; and he was habituated to working with a human partner. Despite our lack of personal warmth, Ghost and I formed a useful two-member pack, with me as alpha and him taking and completing orders with precision.

And by the end of the third week, despite everything both of us could manage, we started to like each other.

Damn it.

At Church's recommendation, I'd created a set of non-standard verbal commands and hand signs. Commands unique to Ghost and me. The more we worked on those, the more Ghost surprised me that he seemed able to understand and retain a higher-than-normal number of them. This made Zan Rosin smile every time she visited our sessions.

"I told you he was an exceptional dog," she said with a smug smile.

I debated telling Ghost to bite her on the ass but restrained myself.

We were working on one set of routines involving oblique-angle gun disarms when Rudy Sanchez came running out of a side door, waving at us. Ghost, who actually *liked* Rudy, suddenly spun and dropped into a fighting crouch between me and Rudy, teeth bared in a very real threat. Rudy skidded to a stop twenty feet away, face going pale, eyes goggling. Protecting the alpha of his pack. Nice.

"Whoa! Whoa, now!"

I said, "Ghost, flat."

It was one of a special vocabulary of code words we'd used every day of the training.

Instantly Ghost's body language changed. He stopped snarling, stood straight, wagged his tail, and pretended to be a charming house puppy that would never hurt a fly. Rudy stayed where he was, not buying any of that.

"What is it?" I asked. "I thought you knew better than to come running out here while I'm with the fur-monster."

"Joe," said Rudy urgently. "They found him."

I didn't have to ask who. There was no one else I wanted found. Veder.

~6~

"What have we got?" I asked Church as I burst into the command center with Ghost and Rudy at my heels.

"CIA sent this five minutes ago," said Church, nodding to the big plasma screen on the wall. There was a picture of a stooped old man buying coffee at a sidewalk café. He looked to be about eighty, with thick glasses and a white frizz of Einstein hair.

I bent close and studied him. A good disguise can turn a rock star into another bland face in the crowd, even to a trained observer.

"That's him," I said.

Church nodded.

"*Dios mio,*" murmured Rudy, and he touched his chest at the place where the crucifix rested against his skin under his shirt.

Behind Veder was a menu board printed in two versions of Danish, one I recognized and one I didn't. Church pointed to the second language. "That's Faroese. It's a Nordic language spoken in the Faroe Islands in the Norwegian Sea. The islands are approximately halfway between Great Britain and Iceland."

"That's where he is?" I asked. "The Faroe Islands?"

"Yes. On Vágar, third largest of the islands."

"When—?" I began, but Church cut me off.

"There's a helo smoking on the deck. You'll take my Learjet straight to Vágar Airport. Langley has a three-man CIA team keeping tabs on Veder. Go!"

Ghost and I ran. Three minutes later we were in the air.

~7~

The CIA spook who met me at the tiny airport on Vágar looked like he was auditioning for the lead role in *Death of a Salesman.* Jowly face, beat-up old suit, scuffed shoes, and morose brown eyes. Not the kind of guy you'd look at and say: "Now there's an international man of mystery."

He watched me give him the once-over and smiled faintly. "I left my dinner jacket in my Aston Martin. Dick Spurlock."

"Joe Ledger."

We shook hands. He had a rock-hard grip with shooter's calluses. Like mine.

"You're not with the Company," he said, not pitching it as a question.

"No."

"Which alphabet are you with?"

I gave him a bland smile. "An off-the-radar one."

He looked momentarily confused, then smiled. "Ah. Let me guess, it begins with a 'D,' ends with an 'S,' and rhymes with 'don't fucking ask.'"

"Something like that," I said, laughing despite myself. I liked Spurlock, even if he was a CIA spook.

Spurlock glanced at Ghost, who was discreetly sniffing him with interest more appropriate to a hungry person reading a diner menu.

"Friendly dog?" asked the agent.

"Not so you'd notice."

"Ah."

We walked out of the small terminal building with the amiable pace of old friends. All for show. His car was parked outside, a five-year-old Toyota with plastic over the rear passenger window.

"Part of the act," said Spurlock. "Nobody looks twice at a down -at-the-heels salesman."

"That's your cover?"

"Only recently," he said as he opened the trunk for me to stow my bags. "My team's been tracking shipments of computer technologies. I'm a mid-level salesman brokering old corporate hard drives for resale to smaller companies. We think that's how a lot of bulk data is moving out of this part of the world, as supposedly wiped hard drives in second-hand computer systems. Guess that's not very interesting to someone like you."

I looked at him for a two-count and he glanced away and cleared his throat.

We got into the car and closed the doors. Ghost flopped down on the back seat.

"Okay," I said, getting right to it, "where is he?"

"A hotel, a new one on the far side of the island. Five-story blockhouse style. Ugly but functional. Elevator in the lobby, interior stairs in the back, two exits. I have men front and back."

Spurlock started the car and pulled into the flow of airport traffic. "He's a smart, slippery bastard. One of my team acquired him when he came out of a bank two days ago. We weren't sure it was him at first, but we managed to get a few photos and ran through a facial recognition program." He cut me a hesitant sideways look. "We…um, we're afraid that he made us even though we have four guys working him, trading off and keeping very low profile. Throughout the day he changed his clothes and disguise three times, and each time we nearly lost him. Guy's a chameleon. First time he was a French businessman and then he was a tourist with cameras and some makeup so that he looked a little Asian. Then he switched to the old man outfit when he checked into his hotel."

"He still there?"

"I called my team while you were clearing customs. No movement."

"What about room service?"

Spurlock cut me another look, more appraising this time, and he nodded to himself. "Twice. Dinner and breakfast. Two different members of hotel staff each time, and we did full verification before and afterward. Veder didn't knock anyone out and slip out the back in a waiter's outfit."

"Not like in the movies," I said with a grin.

"No," he agreed, "but I'll bet that he won't look like an old man when he does leave his room. Like I said, the guy's a chameleon."

We drove for a few minutes in silence as I digested the information.

Eventually Spurlock spoke. "The woman who was killed. Courtland?"

"Major Grace Courtland," I corrected, and he nodded. "What about her?"

"I never met her. Heard some stuff, of course. She was in all the papers after that whole Mengele thing came out. It was like something out of a Michael Crichton novel. Weird. The media painted her as the hero, the one who saved the day."

I said nothing.

"Is that how it happened?"

"What are you saying?" I asked him, my voice cool.

"Hey, no offense, Joe," he said quickly. "It's just that I know how things work in our world. The person who gets the ink isn't always the one who deserves the praise. I just wondered what her role really was."

He was stopped at a light and I turned very slowly to face him. "Grace Courtland was the best woman, the best person I ever knew, and she died in the line of duty. If it wasn't for her, people would be dying in the streets, governments would be blaming each other, and there would be missiles in the air. That is not a joke. You and I are alive because of her and anyone who says different is going to fall right off my Christmas card list, you dig? Anyone who speaks one word against her, or diminishes the value of what she did, will have a whole new set of problems to deal with, starting with a dramatic increase in their medical and dental bills. Am I making myself clear?"

Spurlock stared at me so long the light changed and the cars behind him began to honk. Then he nodded and drove on.

After a minute he said, "I wasn't speaking ill of her. I was asking for the inside scoop. Agent to agent."

I said nothing.

"Some of us are so far out of the loop, so far removed from the action, that nothing we do really matters a damn," he continued. "You mostly never hear about an agent going down in the line of duty, and when you do, and that person makes the papers, you tend to think that there's politics in that. That it's some pencil-neck's idea of spin control from something you'll never be privy to and never understand. And it makes you feel that nothing *you* do matters a wet fart. It's cynical, sure, but there it is."

I said nothing.

"To know that one of *ours*, one of us, did something really big, really important… Well, hell, that makes everything else okay. All the years spent doing scutwork, all of the reports you write that you think no one ever reads, all the loneliness. I'm not saying this right," he admitted and sighed. "It's just nice to know that we actually *won* one, y'know?"

I took a long breath and let it out slowly.

"Yeah," I said. "I know."

"So, no offense, man, okay?"

"None at all."

"Well," he said, "at least we have the bastard cornered. Time for a little bit of payback."

We drove the rest of the way in silence.

The island was green and pretty, but I couldn't care less. Despite the outward show of calm detachment I'd constructed, inside I was going batshit crazy. My head felt like it was full of bees, my gut was sick with greasy sludge. Ghost must have caught some of my nerves and whined quietly. I reached back to pet him, and he licked my fingers. It was the first time he'd ever done that and I found it oddly touching.

At the hotel, Spurlock pulled around back and the three of us got out. The rear street was little more than an alley with dumpsters, a vagrant speaking in Dutch to the pigeons he was feeding, and a nondescript late-model sedan parked by the exit. As we passed the vagrant, Ghost barked at the pigeons, scaring them into flight. The vagrant cursed him and me even though I growled at Ghost to knock it off.

Luckily, I don't speak Faroese, or Dutch for that matter. I'm pretty sure some of his remarks involved me and livestock.

We hurried past him and flanked the car.

Ghost started growling when we were still fifteen feet away, and it had nothing to do with pigeons.

There was no agent behind the wheel.

There was only blood. Ghost sniffed at it and gave a short *whuff*.

Spurlock and I pulled our guns and fanned them up and down the street.

The vagrant suddenly started screaming. Calling for the cops. Maybe calling for God Himself.

"Call your team," I barked, but Spurlock was already speaking into his cuff-mic.

"Henderson! Reed!"

But Henderson and Reed weren't answering, and I knew they never would.

As I approached the exit door, I felt Spurlock move up behind me. He had his gun in a two-hand shooter's grip and his face was set and grim. Ghost was right behind him. Spurlock looked from the dog to the car to me to the door.

"You ready?" I asked.

He licked his lips and nodded.

I pulled the door and stepped back to let him go in first. This was his stakeout and he knew the building. The rear entrance was empty, nothing more than a service door and a short hallway that broke right to the kitchens and left to a set of stairs.

"What floor?" I asked.

"Five." He looked up the stairs. "You go, I'll cover."

I shook my head. "Better if Ghost and I hang back. You know the room, Ghost can watch our backs."

Spurlock hesitated, then nodded. He drew a breath and headed quietly up the stairs. I wondered how scared he was, and how often he'd done this sort of thing. CIA field agents rarely have a James Bond moment; most don't carry guns, and even fewer have used them.

Even so, he was well trained, moving on cat feet as he climbed the steps, positioning himself properly to check his corners and turns, keeping his gun up and out the way he should, and tracking line-of-sight with the mouth of the barrel. I followed in harmony, watching down the stairs even though Ghost was behind me, and checking the fire doors on each landing.

On the fifth floor, Spurlock covered the door and head-signaled me to go first, but I shook him off. His men knew him by sight, but I was a stranger with a gun. Last thing I needed was to walk into a friendly fire incident.

Spurlock snorted and went first. I don't think my caution impressed him much. Maybe I wasn't living up to the DMS super-spy image. He ran down the hallway, taking many small steps instead of large loping ones; it was a balancing trick to keep that natural jolts of running from spoiling aim. I was comforted to see that despite everything, Spurlock remembered all of his training. I'd met a few other CIA spooks who were far less competent.

I came up close behind him, with Ghost right at my heels.

"Which room?" I asked quietly.

"End of the hall."

"Where's your man?"

Spurlock made a face. "I don't know. He should have been in the stairwell where he could watch the hall."

"You have your team on a wire?"

He paused and then met my eyes. "No one's answering."

"Shit," I said, and he nodded.

There was no real cover in the hall, and even the door frames to each of the guest rooms were only a couple of inches deep. So we had to use speed instead of stealth. We put our guns up and ran full-tilt down the hall. I signaled Ghost to stay two paces back and was gratified to see that he was following every one of the commands we'd rehearsed. Yeah, I'll say it. Good dog.

"Kick it," I said. There was no time to explain that I'd had arthroscopic surgery on my knee and ankle after the Jakoby thing. I was weeks away from being able to kick anything. Spurlock shot me another annoyed look, but he kicked the door.

Actually, he kicked the hell out of the door. He used the impetus of his run to launch into a flat-footed kick that struck the wood right beside the knob and ripped the lock out of the frame with a *bang!* and a spray of splinters. He landed in a tight crouch and pivoted on the balls of his feet, sweeping his pistol across the room; I skidded in behind him.

And froze.

Ghost jolted to a stop in the doorway. He stared into the room.

And gave a single, short bark.

I didn't need him to tell me that all of our haste and caution had been a total waste.

The bodies of the three CIA agents told that story with grim eloquence.

~8~

"Jesus Christ," breathed Spurlock. His mouth sagged open and the hands holding his gun drooped slowly until the barrel was pointed uselessly at the blood-spattered carpet.

The room was an efficiency. A bedroom with a full-size bed, one overstuffed chair, a television on a chest of drawers, and a tiny bathroom. No wardrobe, nowhere to hide except inside the bathroom and I sent Ghost in to check. He made his *whuffing* sound and sat in the doorway. All clear.

I stood in the doorway and tried to read the scene. One agent was slumped in a chair, his hands bound with plastic cuffs, a gag tied tightly around his mouth and jaw. There were two black bullet holes above the bridge of his nose. The second agent lay on the floor ten feet inside the room. His hands were not tied and his gun was on the rug a yard from his open fingers. He had one bullet wound above his right eye, and a second in the back of his head. The third agent was right inside the door, bullet holes in his temple and the back of his skull.

In the bathroom doorway, Ghost growled low in his throat, alarmed by the smell of blood and cordite. Spurlock stood in the middle of the room, his pistol down at his side, face slack, eyes moving from one body to the next. He looked like he was a half-step from going into shock.

"Holster your weapon," I said, and Spurlock jumped. When he hesitated, I snapped at him, "This party's over and you're not paying attention to your gun."

He looked at his pistol as if he had no idea what it was, then he slid it into the quick-draw shoulder rig he wore under his grubby suit coat. I put mine away too.

"Check the room," I said. "Check everything. Looks like Veder spotted the man in the hall, lured him here and took him prisoner. Maybe forced him to call the others, maybe kept him alive as a hostage. We'll never know." I moved over to the seated dead man and saw a faint peppering of black powder on the side of the dead man's face and clothes. "Yeah," I said, "the shooter crouched down here, behind the chair, and when the second agent came in, he took him with two shots."

"How do you know that?" asked Spurlock.

I pointed to the gunshot residue on the seated dead man and pointed my hand at an angle to approximate the line of fire. Then I crossed the room, clicked my tongue for Ghost to move, and stepped into the bathroom.

"When the third agent entered the room, Veder took him in the temple from here. Then he finished it with one to the back of the head, turned and put two into the guy in the chair. Small entry wounds, no exits. Probably a .22, maybe with a sound suppressor."

"Assassin's gun of choice," observed Spurlock.

"And Veder should know," I said. "He's supposed to be the best of the best."

Spurlock gave me an enigmatic look. "You sound like you're impressed."

I shook my head. "No. Veder's a rat bastard and I want to blow out his lights," I said. "But you have to admit this was a professional job. If we had any doubts that this was Veder, we don't now." I looked at him. "Look…I'm sorry about your team. Really. I've lost a lot of people on my teams."

He said nothing and his eyes had a totally dead look to them. As if all traces of life and humanity had drained away.

"Really…I'm sorry," I said. "Were you close with these guys?"

Spurlock didn't answer, and I felt like a total jackass.

I cleared my throat. "Okay. Let's toss the room. This all happened between the time you left here to pick me up and now. That's what? Forty minutes? Veder can't have gotten far. Maybe he left in too much of a hurry. Maybe he left something we can use to track him."

Spurlock nodded.

"You start looking," I said, "and I'll call it in."

He lingered there for a moment longer, and then turned away and began searching the room.

I edged toward the door and removed my cell from my pocket. Church answered on the second ring. I explained what happened.

"That's distressing news, Captain," said Church. "I'll arrange to have the airport closed and have our people do a thorough background check on passengers of all flights departing Vágar in the last hour."

"Boats too. I think there's a ferry."

"I'll handle all of that, Captain. I've been moving assets into the area since before you left US airspace. If Veder's there, then he's in a bottle and we *will* find him."

"Yes, we damn well will," I said, and I made sure to pitch my voice loud enough for Spurlock to hear. I wanted him to know that his people mattered too. This wasn't just about my personal vengeance, though in truth—to me, anyway—Grace was all I could think of.

Then I pitched my voice lower. "Look, maybe you should call this in to Langley. Take Spurlock off the hook. He seems like a decent guy, and I'd hate to see him take the heat for a failed mission. It's not his fault that Veder was too much, even for a four-man team."

Church was silent for a moment. "Spurlock's there with you? In earshot?"

"Almost," I said, hoping he'd have the tact not to want to push this conversation any further. Spurlock was probably already wondering to what armpit of the planet his section chief was going to send him. Having an entire team cut out from under you *while* losing your quarry was not exactly a highway to promotion.

"Stay alert, Captain," said Church, and disconnected.

I glanced at Spurlock, who was on his hands and knees, peering under the bed. Ghost was standing next to him, sniffing at the agent and the bed and the blood that seemed to be everywhere.

Spurlock shot me an irritated look.

"Would you please get your dog away from the crime scene," he said coldly. "He's not helping."

"He's trained for—"

"For what?" snapped Spurlock. "Forensic evidence collection?"

"Well, no, but—"

"Then put him in the bathroom before he screws up any chance we have of finding something useful."

I nearly growled back at him, but I reined myself in. The guy had just lost three people he knew, maybe friends. If he wanted to bitch a little bit, I figured he more than earned the right. So, I clicked my tongue for Ghost. I pointed at the doorway and told him to sit. He did, but he contrived to give me a long-suffering look as if to say that idleness was a vast waste of his considerable talents. Or I could have been reading a bit too much into a dog's expression. I was beginning to lose perspective on that.

Ghost watched us both with bottomless brown eyes.

"What did Mr. Church say?" asked Spurlock as he continued to fish under the bed.

"Huh?"

"Your boss? What did he say?"

"Oh…they're closing the airport, cutting off the ferry. Checking manifests and such. The works. We're putting a net over everything. We'll find him."

"Good." Spurlock had his whole arm under the bed. "Tell me something, Joe."

I began opening drawers in the dresser. The top one had two pairs of boxers and two pairs of socks. I checked them, but there was nothing.

"The woman Veder killed—Major Courtland—were you friends?"

I opened the second drawer and found a shaving kit.

"Joe—?"

"Yes," I said softly as I unzipped the kit. "She was a friend."

"A close friend?"

There was no shaving stuff in the kit. Instead I found makeup. Hair dye, several sets of colored contact lenses, false teeth. A high-quality field kit.

"Yes," I said. Very softly.

"I'm sorry."

I nodded and placed the kit on the top of the dresser. In the third drawer I found a dozen passports, a thick wad of currency from five countries, and more make-up. False beards, mustaches, wigs, each in separate plastic bags. There were also two magazines loaded with .22 rounds.

"What'd you say?" I murmured distractedly.

"I said that I was sorry."

I glanced at him.

Spurlock was no longer fishing under the bed. He knelt behind it, and he held a .22 pistol in his hand, the barrel extended by a Trinity sound suppressor.

"Truly sorry," he said.

My mouth went totally dry.

"Veder," I whispered.

"Veder," he agreed.

And fired.

~9~

Three things happened all at once.

I threw myself sideways and the bullet punched a hole through the air so close that it seared a white-hot line across the outside of my ear.

Veder fired a second round.

And Ghost launched himself across the room. Immensely fast, deadly quiet; moving like a white missile from his spot by the door, crossing the small room in the space between the first and second shot, teeth bared as he leapt.

Veder—Jesus Christ, but Veder was fast.

He pivoted in place and whipped the barrel across Ghost's face with terrible speed and power, catching the dog on the temple and tearing a yelp of pain from him. Ghost hit the floor and slid in the blood, but even as he landed his nails tore at the carpet for purchase. He scrabbled around and came right back at Veder, but again the killer was faster. Veder fired two quick shots even as he threw himself backward away from Ghost's fangs. The first shot punched a hole through the drapes; the second clipped Ghost on the shoulder. With a second yelp, louder and sharper than the first, Ghost collapsed backward, blood splashing all over his white fur.

Veder swung around to take me with the next shot, but now I was in motion, driving toward him, leaping across the corner of the bed. I slammed into him with a flying tackle that knocked him off his knees and drove us both all the way to the far wall. The .22 went flying over my shoulder.

We crunched into the wall and I collapsed down on top of him. I was bigger and heavier, and I wanted to snap his bones under me, but Veder was packed with wiry muscles that he'd disguised under the frumpy businessman's suit. He pivoted his hips and drove a two-knuckled punch up under my chin, rocking my head back against the wall. A second punch nearly crushed my windpipe, but I dropped my head, blocking the blow with my chin. Pain detonated along my gum line and I tasted blood in my mouth.

Veder threw himself backward, creating distance between us so he could use his feet. He was good. Really damn good. His first kick caught me on the left shoulder, numbing my arm; the second hit me square in the sternum and that slammed me backward into the wall again and drove a lot of air out of my lungs.

He tried a third kick, but the impact of the last one had shoved him away from me and he didn't have the reach to do more than bruise my chest. I gulped in as much air as I could and kicked out with the point of my toe—not at his body, but at his kicking leg. The reinforced toe of my shoe crunched into his calf, mashing the muscle. I combined off of that, throwing my weight onto my hip and snapped kicks at his ribs, one, two, three, driving a grunt of pain from him.

Veder threw himself away from me and despite the pain he must have been feeling did a neat little backward roll and came out of it on fingers and toes. Then he launched at me. His face did not show a flicker of expression, but instead displayed only a dispassionate—or perhaps disconnected—calm and a professional determination. I'm not even sure I was an enemy so much as I was simply another problem to be solved.

He drove his shoulder into me, catching me mid-thigh and slamming me for a third time into the wall. But I was half-ready for that and as I hit, I dropped my upper body weight straight down, using it to put substantial power into a descending elbow smash which caught him between his shoulder blades. The blow flattened him to the floor, but when I bent over to try and seal the deal with a couple of kidney punches, he swept one leg backward and up in a scorpion kick, catching me right on the forehead.

I hit the wall for the fourth time and fireworks exploded inside my head.

Veder rolled onto his side and used his bent arm to sweep my legs out from under me. I crashed sideways to the ground and he scrambled atop me, pinning my arms to my sides with his thighs while he rained punches down on my face.

I could hear Ghost whimpering and snarling only a few feet away, but I couldn't see him.

The only chance I had was to keep Veder's iron-hard fists away from my eyes and nose, otherwise the pain and disorientation would lose me the fight, my life, and any chance I had at avenging Grace's death.

So I buried my chin down and clamped my teeth onto the soft flesh inside his left thigh. I bit down with all of my rage and Conrad Veder screamed.

He also tried to stand up, to get away from my teeth, and I let him, not that I had much choice—his movement nearly tore half the teeth from my mouth. As he rose, I snapped my foot up and kicked him on the ass, and this time he was the one who hit the wall.

With a growl, I rolled sideways, clipping the inside of his right ankle. Veder toppled over and fell, and even as he was going down, I clawed my way along the inside of his trouser leg until my hip rested on his knee. That gave me the perfect angle and I punched him in the balls as hard as I could.

Veder screamed, a shriek that rose instantly to the ultrasonic.

Agony gave him power though, and he hooked his thumb into the corner of my mouth and tried to tear open my cheek. I had to roll with his pull in order to save my face, and that put me right in the path of his other hand. Two punches battered my temple and eye-socket, and my left eye went completely dark.

Then Veder squirmed out and kicked me away from him.

I covered my face with my arms, expecting another kick but too disoriented to stop it, but there was no blow. I turned in horror to see him crawling toward his fallen pistol. With a cry, I flung myself at him, but I was too far away and he snatched up the gun, turned, swinging the barrel toward me.

Then something blundered past me, white and red and snarling like a demon from Hell.

Conrad Veder screamed again as Ghost leapt at him and clamped his jaws around the wrist holding the pistol. There was a muffled bang as the gun fired, but the bullet punched into the wall a foot away from me. Blood exploded from Veder's wrist and he began pounding on Ghost with his left hand.

I staggered to my feet and half-fell across the room.

"Ghost!" I snapped. "Off!"

With a growl of mingled rage, pain, and frustration, Ghost wrenched himself away from Veder, his fur covered with blood and his eyes totally wild. The gun and the gun-hand were still clamped in his jaws.

Blood jetted from Veder's wrist.

I grabbed him by the hair and hauled him to his feet, then kneed him in the groin, head-butted him, and chopped him across the throat so hard that it jolted my whole body.

There was a big, wet crunching sound in his throat, and Veder staggered away from me, his eyes wide with panic, the fingers of his one remaining hand scrabbling at the total red ruin of his throat. He shambled backward and tripped over the body of one of the dead men and almost fell out the window.

Almost.

I caught him.

I pulled him close and looked deep into his dying eyes. His mouth was trying to form a word. Not "help." Not a plea for mercy. His bloody lips formed a word he had said earlier. And, somehow, here in his last moment, maybe he meant it.

"Sorry."

I stared into his eyes, confused by the word. Disgusted by it. Angered by it.

"Fuck you," I said, and I spat in his face.

Then I shoved him out the window.

Even with a smashed throat he found a way to scream all the way down.

~10~

He missed the car by ten feet.

I leaned out the window and gazed down on the sprawled

body. Waiting for the pain in my head to stop. Waiting for my left eye to start working again. Waiting for sirens.

The eye cleared, but there were no sirens.

It was a back alley in a quiet town on a remote island. No one even noticed.

Ghost limped across the floor to me. He still had the hand in his mouth.

I told him to drop it, and I swear there was a look of disgust on his face when he did so. He whimpered softly and leaned against me.

The bullet had torn a furrow along his side, and—I found out later—notched the bone; but he would heal. He was young and strong, and he would heal. I tore up the sheets and bound his wounds.

Together we limped out of the room and down the back stairs to the alley.

Veder was dead.

It felt weird to think that. To know it.

"Grace," I said.

Ghost whimpered.

It took five minutes to load Veder into the trunk of the car. I was in pretty sorry shape. The keys were in the dead man's pocket. Ghost crawled into the back seat, I got behind the wheel.

For a few minutes I did nothing but sit there with my forehead resting on the steering wheel, feeling the pain. Wondering what I would feel when the pain ended. Veder was dead.

Where was my purpose?

I started the car and we drove out of the town and into the country. I drove aimlessly, unsure of where I was going, unable to read the road signs. The only decisions I made were to steer away from other traffic.

Eventually we found ourselves on a deserted stretch of coastline. Rocky and bare, blasted by the winds and the sun. Bleak.

Perfect.

I dragged Veder's body out of the trunk and kicked it over the edge of the hill. He rolled sixty yards down the slope, halfway to the smashing surf.

There was no shovel in the trunk, just a tire iron. It was enough. I'm not sure I remember digging the hole. I'm not sure why I started.

It was probably stupid, pointless, but I did it anyway, working at it with the relentlessness of madness, chopping into the ground, tearing at the soil, throwing away rocks, repeating, repeating. A task assigned in Hell and completed with insane dedication.

When the hole was deep enough, I tumbled Veder into it. The gun and the gun-hand too. Then I covered it over with dirt and rocks and all of the tons of grief that filled my soul.

Maybe I stood over the grave for ten minutes. Maybe it was an hour. I really couldn't say. I remember the sound of Ghost's nails on the rocks as he limped down the slope to join me. We stood there, battered and bloody. He stared at me while I wept.

"Grace," I said.

The wind blew off of the ocean and scoured the tears from my cheeks.

Veder was dead.

Every law enforcement agency in the world was looking for him. Church wanted him almost as badly as I had. Church would want to see the body.

I stood over the grave and then looked up and down the coastline. It was exactly the same in both directions. If I drove away, I'd never be able to find this place again.

Kind of the point.

I unzipped my pants and pissed on the grave.

Not exactly a marker, but a mark of a kind.

Ghost watched me, his intelligent eyes boring into mine.

I zipped up and turned away. Then I paused at a sound, and I turned to see Ghost pissing a hot stream onto the rocks.

He was a dog, there was no way he could understand why I'd done it. Contempt was not a trait animals could grasp. Right? Besides, he hadn't even known Grace.

Even so, I smiled at him. At the member of my pack.

"Come on, partner," I murmured.

Together, we climbed the long hill back to the car.

~ * ~ * ~

JONATHAN MABERRY is a New York Times bestselling author, 5-time **Bram Stoker Award**-winner, 3-time Scribe Award winner, **Inkpot Award** winner, anthology editor, writing teacher, and comic book writer. His vampire apocalypse book series, **V-**

WARS, was a Netflix original series starring Ian Somerhalder. He writes in multiple genres including suspense, thriller, horror, science fiction, epic fantasy, and action; and he writes for adults, teens and middle grade. His works include the *Joe Ledger* **thrillers,** *Kagen the Damned, Ink, Glimpse, the Rot & Ruin* **series,** *the Dead of Night* **series,** *The Wolfman, X-Files Origins: Devil's Advocate, The Sleepers War* (with Weston Ochse), *NectroTek, Mars One,* and many others. Several of his works are in development for film and TV. He is the editor of high-profile anthologies including *The X-Files, Aliens: Bug Hunt, Out of Tune, Don't Turn out the Lights: A Tribute to Scary Stories to Tell in the Dark, Baker Street Irregulars, Nights of the Living Dead,* and others. His comics include *Black Panther: DoomWar, The Punisher: Naked Kills* and *Bad Blood.* His *Rot & Ruin* young adult novel was adapted into the #1 horror comic on Webtoon and is being developed for film by Alcon Entertainment. He the president of the **International Association of Media Tie-in Writers,** and the editor of *Weird Tales Magazine.*

He lives in San Diego, California.

Find him online at www.jonathanmaberry.com

They're Smuggling What?

Dana Bell

Smells. Unwashed humans. Stale air with a machine smell. Others I did not know.

A hand rested on my head and a soothing voice spoke to me. I understood the words. I'd heard them before. "It's okay."

Gingerly I put my paw on the surface, surprised at how solid it was, and cold.

My human Lisa laughed, warm fingers scratching behind my ear, my favorite spot. "You'll get used to it."

I walked beside her. I didn't know why the humans stared at me. Surely I couldn't be the first 'dog' as we're called, they'd seen.

A door swished open and before me was an office much like I'd seen before. Others in gray uniforms sitting at desks, the rich scent of their favorite drink tickling my nose.

"Officer Jordan," a male called, motioning to my companion.

"Come on, Sammie."

The male frowned when I joined them, sitting down on the hard surface and waiting to see what new orders awaited us.

"I didn't realize you had a K9 partner." I sensed he didn't like me.

"Captain Griggs assured me he'd explained."

With a shrug the other replied, "I'm in charge around here. Been here since the station opened. I'm Mason Lance."

Lisa nodded, her black ponytail bobbing at the motion. "Long time." She inclined her head. "Nice to meet you."

"Twenty years." His eyes, the shade of trees, looked at me. "Our biggest problem here are domestic disputes and smuggling."

"Sounds like a nice change. I'm used to handling worse."

Back on Earth, we'd been part of the homicide team. I hated the smell of blood and death.

"Surprised you and that dog qualified for this post."

"I passed all the tests as did Sammie." She sounded offended.

"Fine." He handed her a computer clip. "Your first assignment."

"Thank you, sir."

"Your desk is in the corner." He turned to look out the

window filled with darkness and sparkling stars. Lisa had explained we'd be living in space. I'd watched with interest from the shuttle while we traveled here.

I laid down as she put the clip on the computer and snorted. "Cats. Someone is smuggling cats."

Cats? Lifting my head I listened with interest.

She smiled at me. "I know you like cats."

My tail thudded. I'd always wanted a cat.

"We'll get your bed and put it on the floor." She shook her head. "If we hadn't been running late-" I knew what she meant. Our shuttle ran behind schedule. I could do without my bed for a little while.

Getting up I looked over her shoulders, my front paws resting on the desk. "Why would anyone be smuggling cats?" she mused, running a finger around her ear like she did when she couldn't figure out a puzzle.

One of the men stopped and grinned at Lisa. "Mel Guest. Welcome." He smelled faintly of a scent I knew. He wore a gray uniform, like everyone else. His hair had been cut short and its odd tinge matched his eyes.

"Good to meet you. I'm Lisa Jordan and this is my partner, Sammie."

"Hi." He rubbed his neck. "German Shepherd?"

"Hybrid. Bred for intelligence and stamina."

He shook his head as if I were a puzzle. "Mice and rats," he explained. "They're avoiding the traps and getting into the food stores." With a chuckle he added, "Guessing someone decided we needed another solution."

"Cats would be a good one."

"Well, they aren't sanctioned by the ruling council. If they catch any, they'll toss them out the airlock."

"That's horrible!"

He leaned closer. "I agree. Good luck."

The next 'day' or so I assumed, there's no sun or moon, we patrolled the corridors. Mostly I needed a long walk and to get familiar with the station with its odd smells. Pretty much the same. White on white. Endless or so it seemed. Except—

I woofed.

"What is it?"

I ran. I heard Lisa's boots on the metal behind me. I rounded the corner and pounced on a man. A box clattered away.

"Get off!" He swung his fist at me, saying words I know to be rude.

A large brown striped cat stood before several of her young. Her tail fluffed and she hissed.

"They aren't supposed to be here." The man glared at me. "I was gonna-"

"I know what you were going to do." Lisa put her hands on her hips. "You'd kill kittens?"

"They're vermin."

"Really?" Kneeling down and careful not to get too close to the angry cat, my human grabbed a tail and pulled out the biggest rat I'd ever seen. "I'd say this creature is more of a danger than mom kitty here and her babies." She showed him the catch. "She killed it."

He shook the box. "My orders are to kill any cat I see."

"Well," she tossed the rat at him. He backed away. The dead rodent hit the floor. "Mom and her kittens are now in police custody."

"You can't do that!"

"Watch me." She took the box away from him and put the kittens inside. He tried to grab the box. "Don't touch them or I'll arrest you."

I growled to make sure he understood.

He glared at Lisa. "I'm gonna talk to Lance."

"You do that."

With a huff, he walked away, the tools around his waist jingling.

Mom cat jumped into the box and began washing her kittens.

"Sorry. Didn't mean to get stinky human on them." Lisa shook her head and picked up the box. "Come on, Sammie."

I grabbed the rat and followed her.

"Why aren't those cats dead?" Mason Lance stalked over to Lisa's desk. I growled, warning him to stay away. He ignored me.

"I will not condone the killing of a mother cat and her kittens.

Besides," she grinned. "Did you see the size of that rat?"

"You left it for me," he accused. His gray uniform had a few dark stains.

"No, Sammie did."

"The dog did?" He glared at me as if I were no better than a rat.

Lisa shrugged. "Sammie likes cats."

"You're supposed to stop the cat smuggling."

That may be our orders, but how to do so shouldn't include killing kittens in my opinion.

"If that rat is any indication and the traps aren't working, the cats are a good solution."

"You don't make policy."

"Who does?"

"The council."

"Fine." She looked at her boss. "When do they meet next?"

"You are going to stop the cat smuggling and toss any you find out the airlock," he ordered my human. I went to her side, waiting to see what he would do. "That's your job."

"One I'm not doing." She crossed her arms over chest. Lisa meant what she said.

"You're suspended."

Her eyes narrowed. I knew that look. "For refusing to kill kittens."

"I don't care if they were puppies!"

How dare he threaten puppies! I took a step forward. "No, Sammie." I knew the tone. I stopped. "That was the wrong thing to say."

"Just a dumb animal," he snarled.

"They understand more than you think."

"Suspend me for not killing cats," Lisa fumed, pacing our quarters. I sat on my bed watching her, while mom cat and her kittens snuggled on the couch. She'd just fed them and was cleaning them.

"Something's not right."

I agreed and yipped, hoping she understood we should investigate.

"You don't suppose," Lisa paused. "Surely not."

She often talked to me. I listened because I understood it helped her solve cases or work out puzzles.

"Sammie, you guard our guests. If anyone tries to hurt them, you know what to do." She gave my head a good scratch. "I'm going to take a walk."

Lisa shouldn't go alone. I rose to go with her. "Sammie, no. Guard." She pointed at the cat and kittens.

Reluctantly I obeyed, howling as she left.

I don't know how long it had been. Mom cat gently touched my nose with her paw and no claws. The kittens were not anywhere to be seen. She went to the door and looked back at me. She wanted me to follow her.

The door swished open and Lisa's boss entered. He made a grab for the cat. She jumped away and hissed. "Where are your kittens, you mangy beast!"

She must have hid them. So well even I didn't know where they were.

I growled. No one entered my territory without an invitation.

"Shut up." He looked around. "Dog doesn't belong on the station."

The cat used her claws on his leg. He yelped. I knocked him down. We ran out the door, the male following us, blood dripping on the deck.

Several tried to stop us, but the cat darted away and a warning snarl from me stopped them. She dashed down a long corridor and stopped outside a door. She yowled loudly.

I heard what I knew to be curses as the human caught up with us. "You want to see, then see."

The door opened. Inside were rows upon rows of human food. Spicy or stale scents reached my nose. Mice and rats were everywhere devouring it.

"You knew." Lisa stepped up behind her boss. "Why?"

He crossed his arms over his puffed-out chest. "You don't need to know."

"Shall I take a guess?"

"You don't want to cross my bosses." His hand drifted to touch his weapon.

"They really want this station to fail?" Her stance indicated Lisa stood battle ready. I waited to see what she might order me to do.

He grinned. "You really think it's that simple?"

"If my guess is so simple, why not just tell me?"

He laughed. "I think instead I'll throw you out the airlock."

A shudder shook the station, followed by several loud explosions. The rodents scampered away, except for one mouse the cat caught, holding it firmly in her mouth.

"What the," more curse words as he sprang out the door so fast he seemed to have forgotten about us.

"Come on, Sammie." Lisa ran. Both me and mom cat hurried to catch up.

We ended up in a room I'd not seen before. Several people were running around, yelling, while one shouted orders. Machines blinked and loud sounds filled the air.

"What happened?" Lance demanded.

"Someone used the thrusters to break our orbit." The human giving orders smelled scared. They all did.

"That wasn't supposed to happen!"

"No, it wasn't." I turned to see Mel Guest, who grinned. "Your little plan to starve out the station so you could use it for raids on Earth backfired. Bosses down there found out."

"You told them."

"Of course I did. Who do you think started smuggling the cats on board?"

"You traitor!" Lance tried to jump Guest. I stopped him and held him on the floor with my body and paws.

"Good girl, Sammie." Lisa pulled her cuffs and secured her boss's wrists. She glanced at Earth receding. "What happens now?"

"We let the cats do their job and the Martian colony will catch us."

"So, they did succeed in establishing one." I heard the wonder in her voice.

For months there had been rumors about an illegal Martian colony. No one knew for sure and it had been a favorite topic during our last assignment.

Mel shook his head. "Not sanctioned. Refugees from all sorts of persecution managed to plant one. They live under the surface so the robots don't see them."

The robots . I'd forgotten about them. They sent back pictures of Mars's surface to the scientists on Earth.

"Sounds like a good place to live." She glanced at her prisoner. "What do we do with him?"

"Oh, he'll prove useful." Mom cat rubbed against Mel's leg. He picked her up. "Thanks for rescuing her." She dropped her mouse in his hand and he put it in his pocket.

"She's yours."

"No. She picked me." Mom cat snuggled into his arms. "Where's her kittens?"

"My quarters."

Hidden but safe. I was sure she'd bring them out when we got back. After all, they needed care.

"Let's lock him up and then I'll release the cats to clean up the rodents. We'll need the food for the journey." His eyes swept the control room. "Keep us on course."

Each nodded and returned to their post.

"The council, I'll bet, will be furious."

He laughed. "Let them. I'm the one who convinced Captain Griggs you and Sammie were needed here. You've got a good track record."

"Glad to hear it." Her hand rested on my head. "What do you say Sammie, excited to live on Mars?"

I barked and wagged my tail.

~ * ~ * ~

Owned by Taj and Esther, her current cat overlords, **Dana Bell** enjoys writing stories including all types of felines. She's written stories about tiger angels, vampire cats and a Serval who travels with a dragon. These tales can be found in *Bast's Chosen Ones and other Cat Adventures.* Her novel. *Winter Awakening* features an all animal cast and *God's Gift* has feline surprises. She has been published in various fanzines, ezines and magazines. She is an award-winning poet and writes paranormal romance under the pen name Belle Blukat.

She lives in Colorado, loves to build and decorate dollhouses, make silk flower arrangements and travel. She can be found at: www.facebook.com/profile.php?id=100047722818013

Horn

DJ Tyrer

"Hey, man, get that thing away from me—I don't like where it's sticking its muzzle," the Elf said as he made vague flapping gestures at the dog busy nosing about his crotch. He added a few words in a Sylvan dialect that sounded beautiful and melodious, in spite of their surely offensive meaning.

Sergeant Axel shrugged his broad Dwarven shoulders and chuckled in unison with the heavy clank of mail.

"*Nobody* likes to have something with fangs poking around a place like that. Just be glad the Chief nixed the suggestion we use Hellhounds. Those things munch on your soul, as well as…"

He nodded to where the dog continued to sniff.

"I'm afraid I'm going to have to ask you to remove your tights."

"You can't demand I do that," the Elf spluttered, "not without a warrant."

The Dwarf held up a scroll in one hand and grasped the dog's collar with the other.

"Warrant," he said, simply, then, "and, if that doesn't do it for you, I'll have Spot, here, remove them for you…"

"Spot?" the Elf whispered.

"Yeah, I know—he's brindled, but, it's a traditional name for the dogs guarding the gates of Dwarven strongholds. Raised him from a pup," Axel added, patting Spot, fondly.

"So," he asked, "DIY, or Spot?"

"Er, I'll have them right off in just a mo'…"

The tights dropped and a leather pouch fell to the floor.

"Whoops!" the Elf exclaimed. "Where did that come from?"

Spot sniffed it and wagged his tail.

"Constable Wheelwright," Axel called, summoning a Human Watchman over, "take this pouch to Professor Edelstein and have him examine the contents."

"Unicorn horn?" the constable asked.

Sergeant Axel nodded and the Elf shuddered. The poaching of unicorn horns was widely loathed and even those whose crimes went no further than the smuggling of the ground end-product into the city tended not to fare too well in the dungeons beneath Hellgate Keep: Even hardened criminals seemed to find the butchery of such pure beings as unicorns reprehensible. And, being a Sylvan Elf, the odds were the Elf had done more than just smuggle it in…

"Oh, and," Axel gave Constable Wheelwright a hard look, "I don't want even a single mote of that stuff to disappear en route to the Professor, right?"

The constable nodded. Watchmen weren't exactly popular inside Hellgate Keep, either.

Then, Axel turned and said, "Somebody recite the prisoner his rights and toss him in a cell. A dirty one."

A Troll lumbered over. "You have no rights, because you are a scummy unicorn killer. You—"

"Somebody who actually remembers the recitation, please!"

"You got it, Sarge." A Human constable, hurried over. "Endellion Greenleaf, you are under arrest for the smuggling of unicorn horn. You have the right to—"

"Come, Spot." Axel headed out of the warehouse, the dog at his heels. At least he could rely on his canine companion for intelligent and effective assistance.

Greenleaf had sung like a bard. And, unlike most bards, whose songs he generally found twee and sentimental in comparison to good old Dwarven drinking songs and war chants, Sergeant Axel had actually been happy to listen to him.

The Elf was up to his pointy ears in the whole poaching and smuggling operation. Knowing he was unlikely to last more than a few minutes inside Hellgate Keep, he had opted to plead for a bargain: Spill his guts, metaphorically rather than literally, and try his luck with Elven justice, instead.

It wasn't that Elves cared any less about unicorn poaching, quite the opposite, in fact, but they had a very chauvinistic attitude towards their own kind, shunning execution and the shedding of Elven blood.

If what Axel had heard was correct, Greenleaf was liable to spend the rest of eternity bound within the trunk of an enchanted oak. The Dwarf wasn't sure that was much of an improvement upon being brutally killed in the corner of your cell, but then, Dwarves had never been that keen on trees, forests, or any sort of nature that existed outside of caves. Probably, Elves felt differently.

Either way, the Chief had agreed to the deal.

Now, they knew every place the smuggling gang used to bring in and distribute their vile product.

At dawn, the Watch would be kicking in a lot of doors—and, Sergeant Axel and Spot would be taking the lead…

"Our people are in position all over the city," Constable Wheelwright said, relaying an imp-borne message.

Watchmembers of all kinds had been conveyed in specially-silenced wagons pulled by muffle-hooved horses to positions close to, but out of sight of, their targets—a variety of inns, taverns, warehouses, hostelries, alchemical shops, and other businesses that served as fronts for distribution—and, as soon as the first blush of dawn appeared upon the eastern horizon and a second round of imps appeared, they would charge in and apprehend all within.

Resistance, as the stock Dark Lord characters of popular drama always declared, would be futile.

"Looks like the sky's beginning to lighten," an officer with a face like a green-skinned pig and a somewhat disconcertingly soft and feminine voice said.

There was a *pop!* and an imp appeared.

"The order is 'go'," it said, before vanishing.

Axel grinned. "We are go. Go! Go! Go!"

With Spot, in his own shirt of mail, leading the way, Axel and his small squad charged towards a fruit-monger's shop Greenleaf had identified as the headquarters of the entire operation.

It only took a few blows of Axel's axe to break down the door and they were inside.

"City Watch! Stay where you are and do not resist!"

A Brownie, busy sweeping up, held its hands up in fright and squeaked in terror as Spot approached.

"Toss him in a bag for questioning later," Axel said, directing his squad further into the shop.

The ground floor appeared, pallets stacked with boxes full of fruit aside, to otherwise be empty, and most of the squad were headed upstairs to arrest the proprietor and other high-ranking smugglers, but Spot seemed interested in a crate of smelly gallaba fruit of the sort that goblins seemed to really love.

Axel wrinkled his nose at the scent and the thought of the sloppy, maggoty insides.

"Sheesh, come away, Spot," he said, reaching for the dog's collar.

Then, he paused and considered. The smell *was* unpleasant, but with the skins intact, not overwhelming.

Spot's sense of smell was far superior to his own, and vastly more discriminating. Wasn't a crate of gallaba fruit just the thing someone might think of to conceal something they didn't want looked at? Most folk wouldn't be too keen to poke around it and you would probably assume it could confuse the nose of a dog…

But, what if the watch-dog's nose was sensitive enough to discern other scents besides the fruit's stench? Was there something hidden in the crate, or behind it?

"What have you found?" he asked Spot as he pulled the crate away from the wall.

Aha—a secret door! Something Greenleaf had forgotten to mention.

It was not even a particularly good secret door at that… If the crate hadn't been in front, even a rather-dense human could have spotted it, Axel was certain.

Carefully, as Spot sniffed at the door with excitement, Axel knelt and examined it. The gang was led by Elves and Elves tended to make a big deal of their culture being full of bows and magic, as if humans and goblins didn't have their fair share of archers and magic users, so he wouldn't be surprised if they'd booby trapped the door with an arrow trap or a hex of some kind.

But, there didn't appear to be any…

Still, he took out the extendable pole he kept in a knapsack on his back and extended it out to its full ten-foot length. Only then, and after a prayer to his ancestors, did he use it to open the door, and then, penetrate the darkness beyond, keeping a firm hold on Spot as he did so.

There was a sudden flash of flame that blinded him for a moment and allowed the dog to pull free from his grasp.

"Spot, return!" he shouted, uselessly.

His ten-foot pole had been reduced to a little over two rather-charred feet in length and his beard was smouldering a little. A fireball—he'd been right to be cautious…

There was shouting and barking from inside the hidden room. Clearly, Spot had caught some criminals.

Axel charged in after him, axe in hand.

"City Watch! Stay where you are and do not resist."

Of course, they did—an arrow pinging off his helmet as he entered the room.

He cursed and took in the scene. There were four Elves, one of whom was already on the floor with a bloody leg and Spot standing over him, growling; a couple more arrows were caught in the mail of the dog's protective shirt, but, Axel was relieved to see, there was no sign of blood.

One of the Elves lunged at the Dwarf with a knife, but Axel just smacked him in the face with the end of his axe-haft, sending him toppling to the floor, unconscious.

"Lay down your—oh, Khazaldak!"

One of the Elves was moving his hands and chanting in the manner of a mage, weaving together magical energies into a spell. Axel had to hope the pendant of protection he wore would be enough to save him.

Spot leapt and bowled the Elf over and stood atop him, jaws perilously close to his throat.

Axel took the opportunity to grab the other Elf, who was still standing, and throw him to the floor. He stood over him and the Elf Spot had bitten earlier and hefted his axe in a threatening manner.

"I don't want any trouble out of you two."

They nodded acknowledgement.

With the other Elf still unconscious from his blow, Axel turned to the would-be spellcaster.

"A mage will be along shortly to render you harmless," he told him. "But, if you're fool enough to try releasing a hex or anything, my partner here will ensure your magical career won't even continue at the level of street conjurer, got that?"

Spot gave a growl and the Elf made a noise like a strangled squeak which Axel took to be a 'yes'.

"Good. The Chief tends to make a fuss when we bring our prisoners back in pieces."

He looked around. Sacks. If they were full of powdered unicorn horn... He smiled, grimly.

There was a sound from behind him and he turned.

"Ah, here you are," he said. It was Constable Wheelwright with some more of his men.

"We've detained everyone upstairs," the constable said. "No horn, though."

"Well, I think I've got a load of it here, plus I've detained what I believed are four of the gang's ringleaders. A good day's haul.

"Now, where's someone who can neutralise this wannabe wizard? I want to get them all back to headquarters ASAP."

As soon as the mage was dealt with, Axel patted his canine companion.

"Well done, Spot. Seems their attempt to magically ward this place against detection did nothing to stop you from sniffing them out. I see a commendation coming your way. Now, let's get back to the Watch-house and have ourselves some breakfast, eh?"

Spot barked in agreement.

~ * ~ * ~

DJ Tyrer is the person behind *Atlantean Publishing* and has been widely published in anthologies and magazines around the world, such as *Insurgence: A Fae Rebellion* (Corrugated Sky), *Tales of the Black Arts* (Hazardous Press), and *Us/Them* and *Crunchy With Ketchup* (both Wolfsinger), and issues of *Fantasia Divinity, Broadswords and Blasters, BFS Horizons, The Fifth Di...*, and *Tales from the Magician's Skull*, and in addition, has a novella available in paperback and on the Kindle, *The Yellow House* (Dunhams Manor).

Visit DJ Tyrer at the following websites:

Author's website – djtyrer.blogspot.co.uk/

Facebook – facebook.com/DJTyrerwriter/

The Atlantean – atlanteanpublishing.wordpress.com/

The Roxy Ruling

Lisa Timpf

Teva peers out the front window at the quiet street, then glances at her wrist chronometer. "It's early, yet, Phoenix." She says the words as though she's reassuring herself.

I pad across the area rug and reach my muzzle up to gently nose her hand. Blessed by the enhanced intelligence granted by my AI implant, I understand what worries her. But being canine rather than human, there are limits to how much I can help. Troubled by these thoughts, I begin to pant.

Teva flashes me a tight smile, tells me I'm a good girl, and scratches behind my left ear. I stretch my mouth into a grin, leaning in to help her reach the right spot.

I'd meant to provide Teva with a distraction, as every line of her posture bespeaks tension. But all too soon, she resumes her anxious pacing back and forth, back and forth, across the living room. I watch, my brow furrowed with worry, noting the dark circles under her eyes.

I wonder now whether it's such a good thing that Rupert insisted on picking us up this morning. Perhaps if Teva were more in control of her own schedule—

The low rumble of a large vehicle slowing as it approaches our driveway interrupts my musings. I woof gently to alert Teva. She looks out the window again. This time, she heaves a sigh of relief. She strides to the foyer, grabs her jacket, and opens the front door so I can dart out into the misty rain.

When Teva and I reach the black SUV, I can see Rupert has opened the hatch for me. I leap into the back of the vehicle to join Sarge, a dark-faced, tawny-coated German Shepherd with aristocratic ears.

Normally I'm more comfortable working with fellow border collies, but Sarge's superior bulk came in handy on several cases we worked together, so he's okay in my books. After we exchange a few quick sniffs by way of greeting, Sarge and I settle in. Sarge positions himself at the right-hand window while I peer vigilantly out the left one. If any vehicles approach too closely on my side, I'll bark to warn them off. Sarge will do the same. It's a self-imposed duty we take seriously. Anything to keep our humans safe.

The trip to headquarters is quiet aside from the steady beat of the windshield wipers as the rain begins to sluice down. I can hear Rupert muttering encouragement to Teva up front. She's replying with mumbled grunts, which become marginally more upbeat until we see the grey brick building of Police Headquarters looming in the distance. Then, both Rupert and Teva fall silent.

Rupert stops the SUV in front of HQ. I think he offered to drive to minimize the length of time Teva would be exposed to the protestors, but I notice with surprise they haven't shown up today. Maybe the rain has dampened their enthusiasm.

I pop to my feet, stretch, and wait for Rupert to open the hatch. I detect a sly grin on Rupert's tanned face as he lifts the tailgate. I stare at him suspiciously for a moment. But his expression isn't a mocking one. Rather, it's as though he's harboring some delightful secret he hasn't let Teva in on.

Teva, Sarge, and I make a break for the door, shoulders hunched against the rain. We reach the overhang without enduring too much of a drenching and wait there for Rupert, who's gone to park the vehicle.

The four of us encounter our first hitch when we stride across the broad marble atrium toward the corridor leading to the Tribunal Hearing Room. A uniformed aide stops us, politely informing Teva and Rupert there'll be a slight delay before this morning's session begins. When I glance at Teva's face, I see that she's biting down on her lower lip. In her fragile emotional state, Teva might easily be derailed by this loop thrown into the schedule. I press against her legs, offering comfort.

Finally, the aide returns. "We're ready now." He speaks with brisk authority. "Follow me."

He leads us down a corridor to a sturdy metal door and swings it open with a flourish. I stop at the entryway, sniffing. I've detected the pungent pong of wet dog and I think, panic-stricken, *I can't stink that much—can I?*

I feel a slick substance on my paw pads. *Water.* A sodden trail leads in from the side door. Clearly, we are not the first to pass this way.

I look ahead. There's a long aisle leading downward, between rows of seats. I prick up my ears. I hear feet shuffling, the crinkle of rain gear rustling.

And I note with relief I am not the source of the smell. Well, not all of it, anyway.

I raise my head and begin to walk down the aisle.

This is a change, alright, from the past two days, and thinking that, I can't help but cast my mind back to the Tribunal's opening session.

The first day of the hearings did not start in an auspicious manner. A crowd of scowling protestors gathered in front of the building greeted us with catcalls and muttered insults.

Then, once we reached the atrium, we met up with Oliver Karm. A former colleague of Teva's who'd since wangled his way into headquarters, Karm offered a sneeringly dismissive opinion of the case she'd chosen to bring forward.

"Are you crazy?" Karm bounced on the balls of his feet as he faced Teva. I noted with satisfaction that he had to look up to meet my handler's gaze—she's got a good four inches on him height-wise. "You know you're blowing up your career, right?" With his hands, Karm mimed debris rising from an explosion. Shaking his head, he strode away.

Thankfully, Rupert, Teva's co-complainant in the case, stepped in. "Ignore Karm. He's a corporate-ladder-climbing jerk, always has been."

"What *are* we doing?" Her green-brown eyes wide, Teva turned toward Rupert.

"We're speaking up for those who can't speak for themselves."

And with that, he led the way to the small meeting room where the Tribunal awaited us.

Behind a sturdy wooden table sat three high-ranking and highly decorated uniformed officers. The woman with dark brown skin seated at the left I recognized as Tashel Morgan. She flashed a tight grin in our direction and offered a gently spoken welcome. Tashel made sure her eye contact included not only the two humans at our table, but Sarge and me as well. I knew from listening to Teva and Rupert's discussions Tashel had served as an officer in the K9 unit earlier in her career. Because of this, I harbored hope she would feel some sympathy for our case.

To the far right sat Chad Lang, his lips compressed into a line as he nodded tightly in our direction.

Occupying center spot at the table, Bruno Weber, Head of the Tribunal, scowled at our small party. Leaning forward on his muscular arms, he addressed his remarks toward Teva and Rupert, ignoring Sarge and me.

"It is your right to bring your case forward to the Tribunal." His acknowledgement came grudgingly. "Yet it is not too late to defer, if you have changed your mind."

Rupert scowled. "We haven't."

"You realize this is your last recourse."

"We do."

With a dissatisfied air, Bruno leaned back. "Then let's begin."

I won't claim that I understood every word. I'm a dog, after all, and the intellectual enhancement provided by the AI implant only goes so far. Besides, some of the chatter seemed as dry as old bones, long buried and not worth gnawing on.

But I caught the gist, and through body language, tone of voice, and scent I sensed the flow of emotion.

I'll keep my recap short, for your benefit.

For over twenty years, select police dogs have been given AI enhancement. This allows them to link to the Cloud to access information. The AI implant also exponentially increases reasoning capability. The Force's current practice calls for mandatory retirement when police dogs reach eight years of service.

And now, the sticky part.

Due to concerns about the AI technology falling into the wrong hands—namely, the hands of criminals—the rules require surgical removal of the AI device at the end of active duty.

I can't say what that removal will actually *feel* like. I haven't been through it. Still, I lived, for a time, with an aging dog who had once been an AI-enhanced operative. While I could see she still seemed something *more* than a normal dog—a trifle keener and more intuitive—I also knew she was less than I, myself.

I still remember the day, seven and a half years ago, when I received the AI implant. The flood of words and images. The ability to sense the nuances of colour. The intoxicating power of logical thought. And overarching all of that, the ability to *understand* those things which heretofore had been mysteries.

And so, when the AI implant is removed, I fear it will be like having a juicy, meat-covered prime rib bone yanked away just when one is poised to enjoy it.

I get chills whenever I think about it.

As a dog, I understand the fundamental concept that any pack must have rules. In the Police Force, there's a process to challenge the rules and to propose new ones. That's what Rupert and Teva are striving to achieve—a change in the rules. Their proposition, quite simply, is this: police dogs should be allowed to retain the AI device after retirement.

I heartily endorse their point of view.

They've stepped through every level, every channel open to them, and been denied each time. The Tribunal is their final recourse.

The point, for me, is far from moot. I am six months away from the eight-year service mark, and so is Rupert's canine partner, Sarge. I suspect it was this pending deadline looming over us all that jump-started Rupert and Teva's decision to move forward with the Tribunal, daunting though it seemed.

On the first day of hearings, the team defending the current practice put forward objection upon objection, some so ridiculous they made me yawn in disdain. They did their best to argue the entire case should be thrown out.

I watched the Tribunal members vigilantly. Tashel took careful notes, her face thoughtful. Chad fixed his silent and slightly disconcerting blue-eyed scrutiny upon whoever was speaking at the time, tapping his fingers on the table impatiently whenever he felt the speaker dallied too long before making their point. Bruno leaned forward when the defense spoke, nodding from time to time.

Of the three, I found Bruno the most intriguing. I tested the air, sensing a hint of the acid odour of fear emanating from him. Yet, glancing around the room, I saw nothing that even remotely suggested a source of menace. During the morning recess, as Sarge and I sniffed the grass and dandelions that made up the patch of lawn behind the building, I asked for his take on it.

"Ambitious, like Karm." Sarge stopped, examined an intriguing patch of grass, then continued. "I've heard Rupert talk about him. Bruno hungers for a higher power, outside the Forces even. Politics. He fears this case'll cause ill will, if public opinion supports the other side."

I nodded, resolving to watch Bruno even more carefully when we returned to the room.

When we arrived on the second day of the hearings, the protestors' numbers had swelled. Teva's pace slowed as we approached the group. Security staff had erected stanchions to keep the crowd back. At least, we wouldn't need to walk directly through them.

"Spend money on humans, not dogs." Teva muttered to Rupert as she read the signs. "The AI program is an abom—oh look, they've spelled that wrong."

"Ignore them." Rupert squared his shoulders and fixed his gaze resolutely forward.

I was about to follow suit when I glimpsed a dark figure on the fringes of that gathering—a man with a mask covering the lower part of his face. Above the fringe of green cloth, the hatred blazing in his eyes made his emotions clear.

I sniffed the air and realized his scent seemed familiar.

I nudged Teva's hand with my muzzle and gestured toward the man. She gasped and tugged Rupert's sleeve, then pointed.

The mask-wearing man turned and fled. Sarge sped after him, traversing the ground in leaps that bespoke his relief in finally being called to physical action.

When we caught up with Sarge and his quarry, the Shepherd was standing on top of the man, whose struggles to escape ceased when Rupert, puffing, caught up with the duo.

"Well, well, interesting to see you here, Mr. King." Rupert crossed his arms.

Corey King had narrowly escaped the net that closed around the Front Street Gang during a raid on a drug warehouse. The Force currently had warrants out for Mr. King on two counts of armed robbery and one of drug trafficking. His capture counted as a significant achievement, and would have been an occasion of celebration had our hearts not been weighted by other matters.

Rupert handed King over to the on-site officers at Headquarters and our small party proceeded to the Tribunal room.

Buoyed by that victory, Teva and Rupert radiated energy as they took their turn presenting arguments for their case. Around mid-morning, Rupert placed a half-dozen devices on a plastic cafeteria tray which he carried to the Tribunal's table.

"What're we looking at here?" Tashel's tone conveyed curiosity.

"One of the arguments against allowing retiring dogs to retain their AI capabilities is fear that the devices will fall into the hands of criminals." Rupert paused for effect. "This tray contains six examples of devices with similar function that are readily available through the underground market. There are more out there."

"Offered for purchase through the dark web?" Chad looked up briefly before returning to his examination of the objects.

"Yes."

"Do our experts concede this technology is equal or superior to ours?" Tashel gestured toward the tray.

"Yes."

"My background's in Information Technology." Chad made the comment quietly. "Just giving these a cursory examination, that wouldn't surprise me."

Rupert turned to Teva, grinning. Before they could present their next argument, though, a tall, lean young man wearing an unadorned uniform entered the room and whispered a message into Bruno Weber's ear.

The head of the Tribunal frowned, rubbed his forehead with his right hand, then stood.

"There's been a development that we need to consider." Bruno spoke in an authoritative tone. "We will recess until tomorrow." Without further explanation, he whirled and left the room, followed by the other members of the Tribunal.

Rupert looked at Teva and shrugged.

I rested my head on my paws, feeling the skin over my brows crease into a worried frown. The recess would leave Teva with time to stew, and that was the last thing she needed.

As if thinking the same thing, Rupert studied Teva's face for a moment, then opened his mouth to say something. He glanced up toward his right, as though pondering. I saw a slight grin quirk the corners of his mouth.

With a jerk of my head, I bring myself back to the present. We've almost reached the front of the room, and it's clear why the smell of wet dog permeates the room.

The lecture hall is filled with uniformed men and women, accompanied by their canine partners.

The room previously allocated for the Tribunal held only a handful of seats for spectators. The number of observers who've shown up for today's session has necessitated a change of venue. That's why we're in the lecture hall, which is normally devoted to training sessions and group presentations.

It's my guess that after seeing Teva's downcast expression at the end of yesterday's session, Rupert called in the troops to show their support. If so, they've responded in spectacular fashion.

As the four of us make our way down the narrow aisle toward the front of the room, the officers stand and salute while their dogs sit, statue-still, beside them. Teva nods acknowledgement and offers a discrete wave when she recognizes a familiar face—which, given how long she's been in the Forces, happens often.

I see Francine Hebert accompanied by her border collie Ginger. *We worked the G'nosi case with her,* I remind myself. And there's Benjamin McDow, from Halifax, Nova Scotia, with his blue heeler, Frisco. And there's—there are too many friends and familiar faces to name. I pace at Teva's left, head high, leaning into her every now and then to let her know I'm there for her.

I glance up at Teva's face. Unshed tears gleam in her eyes, but her chin juts forward with a new resolution. I recognize that expression. She's ready for battle.

As the morning wears on, Teva takes her turn facing the Tribunal.

"One of the reasons we brought this case forward is to stand up for those who can't speak for themselves." She nods toward me, then gestures toward the silent listeners sitting beside their human companions.

"What is the nature of working animals? It is to *work*, to perform a task, that is true." Teva's hands move as she speaks. "Yet we believe we have obligations toward them even after that work is done. After the world wars, many of our service dogs and horses were abandoned overseas, like tools to be discarded when their use was done." She pauses. "And yet, they were living, feeling beings."

"The dogs will still be alive and well cared for after the AI linkage is removed." Chad crosses his arms and frowns. "I don't see the problem."

"They will live diminished lives." Teva's voice trembles with passion. "What right do we have—"

"It's *our* technology." Chad isn't giving up so easily. "We give it, we can take it away."

"Who are we to play God?" Teva's voice rises. Behind me, I sense restlessness. Low growls are uttered and the room takes on an electric quality. My hackles rise of their own accord and I raise my head to glare at Chad.

"Order!" Bruno, the Tribunal leader, commands. Silence blankets the room. Yet that quiet contains an element of menace, like the restless undercurrent of humid summer air before a storm. "There will be a short recess. We resume in ten minutes."

Bruno shoots a glare at Teva, and the message, if unspoken, is clear: when we resume, everyone had better have a grip on their emotions. Or else.

Teva's hands shake as she slumps behind the table.

"Do you have the jump stick?" Rupert's voice is gentle.

Teva nods, rummaging in a uniform pocket before handing him the small red device.

"I'll cue it up. Why don't you take the dogs out for some air?"

Taking the hint, I scramble to my feet. I'm eager to visit the patch of grass behind the building. Maybe by now the rain has stopped. I have to hope that something will brighten Teva's mood.

We're back, now, and the break appears to have calmed the mood. At Rupert's gesture, the lights dim and the intelliscreen at the front of the room brightens.

Images play across the screen's large surface, and though my eyes have some difficulty following them, I can decipher the story well enough.

The images start with a close-up of a border collie pup's face. The camera zooms out to show Teva, her hair dark brown rather than the current salt-and-pepper mix, lifting the pup gently. When the youngster reaches Teva's eye level, the woman whispers, "We're going to be partners, you and I, Roxy."

Roxy. I feel my pulse quicken. *I lived with her for a time, when I first came to work with Teva.*

The video shows Roxy going through the increasing rigors of training. Roxy, with a bright glow in her eyes, the glow of intelligence. Roxy, taking direction and yet also thinking on her own. Roxy, her posture expressing her delight at the wonders of an expanded world.

Roxy, operating at a level that I'd never seen. *That special gleam in her eyes had vanished, by the time I met her.* I suppress a whimper.

Now, the screen shows Roxy prancing beside a young girl. *That's Mia, Teva's daughter.* Mia, who now lives in a downtown apartment and practices law with a small but highly respected firm. Here, though, she is a carefree child dancing to music, and Roxy cavorts beside her, busting moves that compliment Mia's and laughing, laughing, with her pink tongue lolling out of her face.

I glance at the audience, human and canine. They're eating this stuff up. They identify with it to their very fibre.

Then I turn my attention to the Tribunal, whose backs are to us as they look at the screen. Tashel's posture portrays watchful interest, Chad is a mixture of openness and defensiveness, and Bruno—Bruno is steadfastly inarticulate as far as his body language is concerned, as if carefully schooling his gestures, like a poker player.

Like summer blending into autumn, the images change.

A party, a gathering of officers and dogs at the Precinct. A cake and a tin of dog biscuits. Farewell pats.

Roxy's retirement.

And then, the final images. The camera shakes, sometimes, as if some extreme emotion held the videographer in its grip.

I'd always known Roxy to be different from myself. But seeing the contrast juxtaposed so closely, through the images— After the device is removed, Roxy's eyes appear duller. Human conversation that would have been followed with ease is now met with a cocked head and a goofy expression. When Mia goes out to play with Roxy, the girl throws the ball and Roxy brings it back. Throw and retrieve, throw and retrieve.

Would it be fair to say there is no joy? No. It would not. I knew Roxy to be a bright, if subdued, spirit. Even the audience can see Roxy's tail is high, and her posture bespeaks simple pleasure.

But it is also clear Roxy is seeing the world through a different lens, and the world she experiences is neither as rich nor as complex as she once found it.

The screen fades to black. In the background, canines whine and humans sniffle as the audience struggles for composure.

"She doesn't look unhappy." Chad spreads his hands, palms upward, as he makes that protest.

Teva reluctantly concedes his point. "It's in a dog's nature to make the best of things." She pauses. "But can't you see how she has fundamentally *changed?*"

"The Tribunal will recess to consider the material presented." Bruno's tone gives nothing away. "We will return when we are ready to present our findings."

There's a steady hum of conversation in the background as we wait. Teva rests her arms against the table in front of her. She slumps, her posture indicating how much emotional strain she's endured simply watching the video.

Suddenly, the buzz of chatter stops, as if someone has hit a sound control.

The Tribunal files in and I study their faces. I *think* I see Tashel wink in my direction and I thump my tail hopefully, just once, against the floor.

Bruno clears his throat, sensing the attention of the crowd upon him. He squares his shoulders and his voice sounds sonorous as he begins to speak. I feel as though I am caught in a spell, and at this moment I can firmly believe Sarge's assertion that Bruno aspires to be more.

"We are now ready to render our decision." Bruno relishes his moment in the spotlight, that is clear. "We applaud Officers Teva Perry and Rupert Melvin for bringing their case forward. After deliberation, we rule that the practice of removing the AI device from retiring police dogs—"

By now, the tension is so thick you could cut through it with the swipe of a dull dewclaw, and yet Bruno pauses there, as though to ratchet things up one more notch. Finally, like a dam bursting under the inexorable pressure of a flood, he renders the Tribunal's conclusion. "The practice should be *stopped.* From this day forward—"

Whatever he would have said next is drowned out by whistling, hollering, and woofing. When I glance behind me, human officers are exchanging hugs. Canine operatives yip excitedly, prancing in place. Then the assembled officers, facing forward, salute Teva and Rupert with a full minute of sustained applause.

Bruno sits, finally allowing a grin to crack his face. Tashel, in turn, stands, and a respectful silence falls once again. "We also concur that this decision will be referred to as The Roxy Ruling."

If she intends that remark to restore order, she has grievously misjudged her audience. Pandemonium reigns once more. No one seems to care.

After a time, the bedlam subsides to a buzz. This is followed by coats rustling, keys jingling, and paws and feet shuffling—the myriad small sounds of a large group of people and animals preparing for departure.

Bruno approaches our table. "No hard feelings, I hope?" He shakes hands with Rupert, then Teva. He is all politician now, and if there were babies or puppies handy, I am certain he would be puckering up even now.

Bruno's expression turns rueful. "My ten-year-old daughter caught my wife and I talking about the case after supper last night, and boy, did she give me grief that we were even *discussing* this issue, as opposed to just changing the rule." He rolls his eyes, and Teva and Rupert chuckle. "She'll be happy to hear the outcome. It'll keep *me* out of the doghouse at home."

"By the way." Chad arrives to shake hands as well. "The reason we cancelled yesterday's session was to look into some information regarding the protestors. It appears the Front Street Gang and their counterparts, working together for a change, staged the whole thing. They wanted to create an impression that public opinion opposed the existence of the AI-enhanced dog program." Chad shakes his head. "Actual opinion polls show us nothing could be further from the truth."

I dart a glance toward Bruno. *So that's why he seems so relaxed now!* I allow myself to wonder, just for a moment, whether he would have fought harder against the decision if he still feared public opinion opposed our existence. I shake myself, as if in so doing I can loosen the thought, send it flying free from my mind. *It doesn't matter,* I tell myself.

Tashel makes her way over, her expression thoughtful. "Thank you for bringing this case forward." Her voice is heavy with emotion. "I just wish—"

"I know." Teva smiles, offering support. I'm sure she's thinking of Tashel's German Shepherd, Atticus, who endured the same post-retirement surgery as Roxy. "I know."

The Tribunal departs. Rupert moves toward the aisle, to make his way back to the Atrium. Teva stands for a moment, gathering her composure, then follows.

Me, I am thoughtful as I trail behind them with Sarge pacing at my side. I think about my own pending retirement, which clearly now is no longer something I need to dread. I find it pleasant to think I will still be *myself*, as I am.

I take a quick glance around. There's no-one behind me. And so I express my delight by performing three tight circles, as though I am chasing my tail, my feet flying faster and faster—

I stop, swaying and dizzy, as Sarge glances back over his shoulder.

I grin at him, then offer a play-bow. "Race you to the humans."

Before he can answer, I'm off.

We catch up with Teva and Rupert just in time for them to hold the door open for us, and before stepping into the Atrium we adjust our pace so that we might seem, to the casual observer, to be models of decorum.

Through the large windows I can see sunlight has won out over the morning's clouds and rain. The marble-floored reception area is packed with people and cavorting dogs. I use nose and eyes to scan the crowd, seeking Ginger and Frisco. It's time to catch up with old friends. Old friends who I will continue to remember, even after my years of service are over.

And with that thought, I perform one more tail-chasing circuit, out of pure joy. This time, I don't care who might be watching.

~ * ~ * ~

Lisa Timpf is a retired HR and communications professional who lives in Simcoe, Ontario, Canada. Her speculative fiction has appeared in a variety of venues, including *New Myths*, *Future Days*, *From a Cat's View*, and *Acceptance: Stories at the Centre of Us*. Lisa's speculative haibun collection, *In Days to Come*, is available from Hiraeth Publishing. You can find out more about Lisa's writing at lisatimpf.blogspot.com/.

Teamwork

Bailey Finn

Detective Jones beat the morning alarm and dismissed it before it had the chance to go off. Down the hall, he could hear the automatic revving of the coffee machine making his morning brew. He got up and found his eight-year-old Belgian Malinois and partner, Odin, at the edge of the bed. He was stretched out with his belly up, half under the bed itself. Jones knelt down and gently shook Odin's belly. "Morning bud, you ready for another day? It's a big one after all."

Odin rolled onto his belly and stretched again before barking in affirmation and wagging his tail. Jones slipped on his hiking gear and refilled Odin's bowl.

"Better eat quick, we gotta get going if we're gonna make the hike." Jones drank the fresh coffee as Odin indulged in his adult large breed athletic mix.

"You ready buddy? Let's go," Jones gestured to the door and Odin barked in agreement. The sun hadn't risen yet as they loaded up in their pickup and drove off to the city park. Odin maintained a heel position with Jones' running pace. When they arrived back at the pickup, Odin whined.

"Hey, none of that, I know it's not the mountains, but we have work today. Don't worry we'll have a longer walk starting tomorrow, and we won't have to wait for the weekend anymore."

Jones loaded up Odin and they drove off again. Jones could tell weekends were Odin's favorite, because there was always a visible difference when Odin got to go with him into the mountains for full weekends as opposed to an hour at the city park. Odin gave a small murmur in response.

"Keep talking back and we won't stop for a second breakfast at the Cyprus Café." Odin licked his lips, gave a bark and took his place in the truck without further complaints. Jones pulled through the drive-through and ordered a hatch chili egg scramble for himself and a cup of whipped creme for Odin. Odin waited for the command to consume the treat, then inhaled it with gusto.

"Atta boy, eat up, we got work to do." Jones patted his companion's head and put his K9 Unit vest on. The change in Odin's demeanor was immediate. Odin sat in his place alert and steady with an elite focus for the rest of the car ride. Once they arrived at the unit Jones parked and set Odin up in the K9 kennel.

"I'll be back to grab you for the party, behave bud." Jones locked the crate and hurried along to his morning briefing. The room was already filling up with other members of the K9 unit and patrol. There was Inrya, an energetic patrol officer who'd been working towards the K9 unit and was scheduled to take Jones's open slot after his retirement. Sergeant Williard was at the front of the table, Charlie, another K9 handler, was finishing the last of a power protein shake as she reviewed notes.

"Hey Jones, there you are. You ready for your last day?"

"Morning. You bet, even more ready for the party. Everyone knows retirement parties are the best. There's always leftover cake for the unit too." The table had a round of chuckles and agreements before the sergeant brought attention back to the assignments of the day. Jones didn't have assignments but instead was on standby for backup and had a mountain of paperwork to complete before the end of the day. Around noon, everyone came back together in the breakroom and the connected conference room to celebrate Jones's retirement. Odin got to participate as well. The sheet cake had both their names on it. Sergeant Williard presented Jones with a unit coin. And the group pitched together for an engraved silver compass and a fully stocked high-grade backpack. The party was filled with laughter, conversation, and stories throughout the years.

"Congratulations on the early retirement, you definitely earned it." Inrya soft-punched his shoulder.

"Yeah, congrats on the promotion by the way."

"Thanks, I'm really excited to be working with Odin. I guess they made the cake before the final decision, huh?" She patted Odin, who was obediently laying by Jones.

"Pardon?" Jones stopped midway through taking another bite of cake.

"Well, you know, he's my assignment partner."

"I'm afraid you must be mistaken; he's retiring with me. I've been processing the paperwork for months."

"Oh, well I got an email this morning." Officer Inrya stood back up, "Don't worry. We can sort this out with Williard."

"Yes, because I am sure that—" Jones was interrupted as Charlie came up to them both looking frazzled.

"Hey sorry to interrupt, but I've lost my access card. Between the party and all my assignments, I must've dropped it somewhere. Have you guys seen it?"

"No, sorry Charlie." Jones shook his head.

"Haven't seen it." Inrya agreed.

"Thanks anyway." Charlie left and made rounds asking others at the party.

"Come on, we'll go straighten this out." Inrya nudged her head in the direction of Williard.

Jones picked up his backpack and compass and joined Inrya to confront the sergeant. Odin followed suit.

"Hey Sarge, you have a minute?"

"Of course, how can I help you two?"

"Officer Inrya states you had assigned Odin to her?"

Williard frowned and rubbed the back of his neck.

"Yeah, I got the confirmation email from the board this morning after the briefing. They decided to reject his retirement. They are keeping Odin on. I am sorry Jones, I just wanted you to enjoy the party at least."

"They can't do that. Today is his retirement date! That kind of notice is unacceptable!"

"Apparently they can, they say he's still got a lot of years left in him for service and retiring him early without reason would be too great of a financial loss." Williard spoke gently.

"I've raised him since he was two months old, that's the reason! His house is my house, his routine is my routine, and his retirement is my retirement! That is my dog, Sarge. Inrya can get one of the new pups to bond with. I can even help fund the financial difference."

"I wouldn't mind that, Sarge. There are plenty of pups in need of adoption. If we start young enough, I could train any of them. If they fail the training, it wouldn't be any different than the regular dropouts," Inrya said.

Williard pinched the bridge of his nose. "With all due respect Jones and Inrya, it's not your call to make. Odin is city property. The board has made its decision. The best I can do is continue to push for his retirement and notify you when it's approved. I know he means a lot, but he's in good hands. The best thing you guys can do is to get Odin acclimated to Inrya. If you want to discuss this further, we should take it to my office."

Jones clenched his fists, and he felt a fire rise up in him. Inrya put her hand on his shoulder. Jones could tell by the pressure she used she was either preparing to hold him back, if necessary or suppressing her own anger. Jones chose to believe it was the latter, if not both.

"Yes, Sergeant." Jones managed to grimace.

"Great, you are dismissed. I'll see you at end of the day for your badge." Williard left first.

"Come on, looks like everyone is headed back to work anyway. We might as well try to make this transition easier on Odin." Inrya suggested.

"Yeah. Okay."

The two of them left the party with Odin in tow to the kennels. Most of the walk was filled with awkward grade-school silence.

"Ya know, it's not his fault. You know the sergeant tried his best."

"He should have told me when he found out."

"Yeah, probably," Inrya agreed, "but no one is perfect." She gave Odin an order to which Odin looked confused and looked to Jones for direction. Jones had to encourage Odin as well as repeat a few orders.

"Go ahead and keep going, he'll get used to it. He might need to be taken off duty temporarily as he gets used to you, though."

"Maybe. I'm sorry. You know we'd do anything to help you out, right? This team really cares about you."

"Yeah, it's a good group. I just wish the board could see Odin and I need each other."

"I know." She gave Odin another command and Odin followed it with a bit more ease.

"I don't mind having him visit or going on one of your hikes with him, at least until this whole thing gets sorted out."

"Thanks, Inrya, it means a lot."

The team continued to train drills until the end of the day.

"I suppose we better say goodbye now. I'll bring you his stuff from home in the morning, in the meantime, there are emergency meal rations in his kennel locker for late nights."

"Good luck Jones, you'll come up with something. We'll be

behind you when you do." Inrya leashed Odin, causing him to tilt his head and once more look at Jones for a command.

"It's okay boy, go on. I have stuff to do, but I'll catch up."

Odin whined but followed his orders as Inrya took him back to the lockers. Odin repeatedly looked back or lost his traditional uniform pace along the way and his whines grew louder the farther away they got. Once out of sight, Jones swallowed the lump that had formed in his throat and gathered up his belongings from his desk back in the main building.

His cubical was modest, it was between Charlie and the next unit in the department. He put everything that was his in a cardboard box. Among the items were his new backpack and compass, his personal stash of office snacks, and a handful of photos of him and Odin. They had taken them every year and on special occasions. He was looking at the photo they had taken during training. Odin couldn't even fit in the vest yet, sleeping on the job. There was also a ball for Odin that still smelt of treats and slobber. Jones reached for the ball when it rolled off and under his desk, closest to the cubical wall. He knelt to retrieve it when he saw an access keycard next to the ball. Charlie's missing card. He picked both the card and ball up and stared at them. Something deep inside him snapped. He had asked for months through the proper channels to retain ownership of Odin to no avail. He had no faith they'd return Odin to him anytime soon. So instead, he would stop asking. Jones resolved to use Charlie's access card to get back into the building and take Odin back by force if necessary. The thought of betraying his unit made him nauseated, but this was for Odin. Jones stuck the extra access card into his box of belongings, covering it with the photos and ball. He then took the box to Williard's office.

"Here's my badge, access card, and my gun. I'll return the uniform tomorrow." He spoke rigidly and made an effort to keep his tone even.

"Thank you, Jones, how are you holding up?"

"I have a plan, sir, don't worry. Thank you for your time."

"Well, I'm glad you are doing better than this morning. I really am sorry; I'll continue to try to negotiate with the board. Thank you for your service, Jones."

Jones simply nodded tensely and left as quickly as he could.

When he arrived home, he found the apartment empty and

significantly drearier without Odin. It was the first night Jones was alone in eight years. He shook his head and resolved to start getting ready for the morning. He got one of his freezer-prepped meals, a chicken and vegetable casserole, and preheated the oven. As the oven heated his dinner, he gathered Odin's food, bed, and toy basket. Then came the camping materials they had used so often on their full weekend hikes: a tent, water purifier, canteen, potable water, campfire cook set, and survival kit. Finally, he packed his own belongings. He left the box from the office in the truck too as he loaded up all the other things he would need to start over.

He took a break to eat dinner, then he went online. He canceled next year's lease. He cleaned up the mess from dinner and showered. He struggled to sleep, wondering if this ambitious scheme would work. It had to work. If he failed, he'd probably be arrested and charged. He'd never see Odin again. When he did sleep it wasn't restful and in the morning he rose early. He drove to the bank and withdrew the entirety of his account. Finally, he tested routes to the mountains they had done weekend hikes on so many times before. When he was satisfied, he made one last stop at the gas station and filled up the tank before heading back to the unit.

Jones buzzed through the building. He didn't bother hiding his face. They already knew him, and once they found Odin missing, they would know he was the only one with the motive and access to pull something like this off. Jones steadied himself and headed towards the kennels. Inrya would have put Odin in the kennels by now and be back at her office based on the schedule. He walked through the kennels. The dogs would bark and howl but there were no handlers present. He stopped at Odin who was waiting at the door eagerly, recognizing Jones without fail. Jones unlocked the crate as Odin wagged his tail, struggling to remain professionally seated. He hugged Odin and pet him as Odin pounced and pinned him, smothering him with slobber.

"Okay. Okay, down boy. You ready bud, let's move." He got up off the ground, removed the K9 unit vest and Odin licked his hand before they ran off.

Jones loaded Odin up in the truck and sped off before anyone became wiser.

He pulled off to one of the hiking parking spaces close to the city limit and ditched the uniform in exchange for his hiking clothes.

Then he continued to drive to another set of hiking trails that went through the mountains. He unloaded the truck and wore everything he could with the new backpack.

"I hope you're ready Odin. This weekend's hike is going to last much longer. But I think we can make it."

Odin barked in affirmation, and they trekked another four hours into the woods off beaten paths and a few ravines. Switching directions and doing all they could to put distance between themselves and the city. After a few hours, they broke for a rest.

"Drink up pal, you've done well" He poured some potable water into Odin's bowl. As Odin quenched his thirst Jones looked through the backpack he was given for the compass. He found the compass next to the retirement card. Jones opened it while waiting for Odin to finish his drink. The card was filled with affirmations. Charlie wrote *'Good luck wherever you end up.'* If only she knew. Inrya wrote *'Don't lose your way'* and Williard wrote *'I wish you and Odin a lifetime of happiness in your retirement. Stay safe on your next adventure.'*

That piqued Jones's interest. Why would he write that if he knew the board denied Odin's retirement? Maybe he signed it before he found out. Jones put the card back and packed up the water bowl, he drank some water himself from the canteen and they continued on.

As Odin and Jones went deeper into the woods, making their way to the other side of the mountains, Jones kept on thinking about the card. What's more, Jones considered it had been awfully simple to get Odin back. There wasn't a single handler on duty and the access card was awfully lucky. Jones wondered if Charlie really lost her access card yesterday, or if the compass and backpack were just because everyone knew he loved hiking with Odin. It was almost as if his team wanted him to succeed. As they wound down at the end of their daily trek and Jones set up the tent, Jones also recalled something Williard and Inrya had told him. They had both said they'd be with us and do everything in their power to help. Odin rolled onto his back and Jones gently shook his belly.

"They let us go, bud. We really do have a great team."

~ * ~ * ~

Bailey Finn is a speculative fiction author who enjoys paranormal adventures and mysteries. She works full time in crisis intervention helping families through the worst of times. When Bailey is not helping those in need, she enjoys ballroom dancing and getting the gang together for a round of tabletop gaming.

Bailey resides in Colorado Springs and is a member of Pikes Peak Writers where she is always happy to connect with fellow authors and readers, as well as dancers and gamers.

The K9 of Spellstruck Academy

Kendra Petresky

SNIFF, SNIFF. Buddy, my Golden Retriever, was on top of me a minute before my alarm was scheduled to fly around the bedroom. Courtesy of a magician from the Spellstruck Supernatural Academy, who specializes in the element of air.

"Okay, boy, your internal clock is a little *too good*," I chuckled. "If I'm gonna have the energy to wrangle the kids today, I'll need my cup of joe."

Rolling out of bed with me, Buddy barked in agreement and led me to the kitchen. With the snap of a finger, the stove sparked on—a gift from another student specializing in fire—and my kettle started boiling the water in less than a minute.

"We've got our work cut out for us today, Bud," I told my trusty K9 as I poured his food in a flying bowl that had "Nom Nom" written across it. "The kids in the Magical Beasts department are training new pets today, and you'll need to be on high alert to guard our amateur magicians in case a creature goes full-blown rogue."

I remembered the last time Buddy and I were on Magical Beasts duty and winced. A baby fire-breathing dragon with six heads had trouble following the magician's lead and ended up burning his robe to ashes. Thankfully, Buddy nipped the boy's feet enough for him to retreat before the dragon could harm him.

Pouring the water over the coffee grounds, I smelled the fresh brew and listened to the sounds of Buddy chomping down and the birds chirping outside while the sun rose over the sparkling snowy hills in my backyard.

It took a mere two minutes for Buddy to finish his food, and I headed back to the bedroom to pull my school resource officer uniform on. Spellstruck custom made my uniform with dark blue fireproof, water-resistant thread. I threw my ballistic vest on top and added my handgun and taser to my belt.

When I got to the front door, Buddy was patiently waiting, sitting by his leash and staring up at me with those big brown eyes. I gave him a quick kiss on the head and led him out the front door.

Professor Winnow was already on my sidewalk with her wand, ready to spawn a portal for us to travel to the academy. Two years of doing this and it never gets old. Buddy always barks in excitement the moment he sees the wand lift and the sparkles start forming around the circular portal.

Of course, to alleviate the suspicions of my magic-less neighbors, Winnow disguises us beforehand by casting a glamor that makes us appear to be stepping into our car rather than stepping into nothingness and disappearing. She then has the car self-drive with a projected double of me down the street and disappear into the woods for the day. I always marveled at her creativity.

Upon arrival at the academy, the grassy plains are littered with random objects–building blocks, ribbons, socks, and scarves. "Excuse the mess." Winnow sighed as she led us through the large black gates. "The Manifesting Magicians were practicing a new spell after school yesterday that allowed them to call forth random items from their bedrooms. It appears they never cleaned up after themselves."

Buddy grabbed a sock in his mouth, but at the snap of a finger, he dropped it. Though mischievous, he was an obedient and trustworthy companion.

"Actually, we wouldn't mind Buddy's help, Officer Chinnagen." Winnow smiled. "Here's a bag."

Of course, the bag was a magical pit when I opened it, likely leading to the exact origin of these objects. I picked up a sock and handed it to Buddy. "Here, boy, you can have it now!" He looked at me with wide eyes for a moment and then yanked it out of my hand. "Now put it in here," I said as I held the bag open for him. He dropped it right in. "Good boy!"

Between Buddy and I, we had the lawn cleaned up within five minutes. "Many thanks, Buddy–you're such a good helper!" Professor Winnow scratched his head and he licked her.

We continued through the large double doors of Spellstruck and traveled to the right, down the hall, and stopped at a steel door with the sign "Magical Beasts Dept." There was a shimmery mist leaking out of the door frame.

"Good luck in there today," Winnow said. "We brought in a new baby dragon this morning and it's full of unpredictable energy!"

She scanned us in with her badge and we were greeted by two young magicians, Fay and Cal, second-year students who were only 6 years old. "Buddy!" They always hugged the dog before they acknowledged me. I loved it that way—attention was not something I liked.

My baseball cap almost blew off from the plethora of baby flying dragons overhead. Thankfully, these weren't the fire-breathing type. Buddy's nose suddenly went berserk, and he yanked the leash, with me running behind him, all the way to a backpack on bleachers to our left.

"Hey!" Cal yelled across the room, frantically running toward us. "I have dog treats in there along with my spellbooks–I'll give him treats later. Come on, Officer C, watch me tame a dragon!"

Though the backpack, especially considering Buddy's reaction, still seemed suspicious, my gaze was immediately averted when I heard Cal yelling and running away from a dragon. "M…My wand broke! Officer C, I have a backup in my satchel next to my backpack! Hurry!"

I tore open his satchel and threw him the wand.

"Raya, Tutum, Tali!" Cal chanted at the dragon and the reptile immediately sat, panting like a dog. Buddy ran up to the dragon and licked him, but now that the chaos had subsided, he ran back to the backpack and continued to sniff relentlessly.

"Cal, I'm going to need to search your backpack. Buddy might be smelling the treats, but I have to make sure," I said as I unzipped it and looked under the spellbooks. I found a loaded gun at the bottom.

Shaken at the discovery, I quickly radioed Professor Winnow and pressed the Big Red Button, which summons a flying white horse to transport students to the Holding Area of the academy. The horse walked through a portal, grabbed Cal's tunic with its mouth, and flung him on his back. Cal grabbed the horse's mane tightly as they flew back into the portal and I stepped through it after them with the backpack.

In the holding area, Buddy continued sniffing and barking at the backpack. I handed it to Professor Glangow, who quickly left campus with the illegal weapon to dispose of it.

I looked at Cal with serious and concerned eyes.

"How did you get this gun, Cal?"

"I—I took it from my Mom's dresser in her room."

"Why did you take it?"

"I was mad at Fay. B—But I wasn't going to use it! I just was gonna show it to her!"

He started crying.

"Cal, we have to take this very seriously. Because of the seriousness of your actions you will be restricted to the hospital wing of the academy for mental health evaluation, observation and treatment, for the foreseeable future, and you will work under the close scrutiny of Professor Shadow. You will be allowed to play with other kids at the hospital during breaks in treatment and schooling there."

Cal was wide-eyed and shaking. Professor Shadow was feared by all the students at Spellstruck, not only because of his scarred face, but also because of the snake he wrapped around his neck who bit students who fell out of line. The snake even stayed in the students' shared dormitory room at the hospital to watch over them while they slept.

Shadow led Cal out of the room, and I took a deep breath while I looked to Buddy. "You saved the day again, pal. Who knows what could have happened had you not found that gun. I'm so proud of you." I scratched his belly, and he rolled over in excitement.

I radioed the police chief from the Spellstruck Police Department, as well as an attorney for the school, and they arrived immediately to discuss disciplinary action for Cal's offense.

"Thank you, Chief Rino and Attorney Jen, for joining me so quickly," I said. "We had a situation where a six-year-old student from the academy brought a loaded gun to school. What are your recommendations for punishment? For now I've sent Cal to the hospital wing for evaluation and Professor Glangow disposed of the weapon, but should he be criminally charged for this offense?"

"I don't think it's appropriate for a six-year-old to be criminally charged at all, due to a lack of culpability," Jen said. "Legally, the child is too young to actually understand what they were doing or the consequences. Not to mention they definitely wouldn't understand the criminal justice system and therefore cannot stand trial and comprehend what is happening."

"I agree with Jen," Chief Rino said. "However, we can investigate Cal's parents for possibly putting the child at risk, and depending on the details, the parents could be charged with child endangerment or other crimes."

"Hmm," I said. "Thank you both for your input. I will have a meeting with Cal's parents as soon as possible to investigate how this happened."

They both nodded and portaled away while I started dialing the number to reach Cal's mother.

"Hello, this is Sarah Bartley."

"Hello, this is Officer Chinnagen at Spellstruck Academy. I'm calling to inform you that we had an incident involving your son, Cal. He is okay, but given the nature of what happened, he was transferred to our hospital wing."

"What happened? What did he do?"

"We found a weapon in his backpack, but I'll need to go over more detailed information with you in person. How quickly can you get to the academy?"

"I'll leave work immediately and I'm going to phone my husband to meet me there. I should be able to get there in thirty minutes."

"Thank you, ma'am."

I called Professor Winnow in to meet with her next.

"In light of what happened, professor, I think we need to seriously increase security," I said.

"What are you proposing?" Winnow asked.

"At the very least, we need to carefully search every dormitory room of this boarding school so we will know if a student is storing a weapon here. And we should also put metal detectors at all entrances to the school in case any outsiders are illegally armed."

"All right; I think that's reasonable. I'll contact some companies and get quotes for how much that will cost as well as see if there are magical methods available. Thank you, Officer Chinnagen. For everything."

Stepping back through the portal left open from the Magical Beasts department, I found Fay sitting in a corner, hunched over and crying. Buddy ran up to her and licked her. "What's wrong, Fay? Why aren't you training with the rest of the students?" I looked around at the five magicians flying around with pet dragons while Professor Renaldo shouted instructions to them.

"Cal hit me yesterday and called me a loser. Why did he have a gun? Am I safe? I don't feel safe." She was crying now.

"Fay, I spoke to Professor Winnow about searching every dormitory room as well as putting metal detectors at the entrances to the Academy. I will make sure you are safe here. Don't worry." I put a hand on her shoulder.

"Come on—Buddy wants to show you a new trick he learned," I said to Fay as I grabbed a treat out of my pocket.

She raised her head up to watch as I threw a treat in the air and waved my hand in a circle. Buddy backflipped and caught the treat in his mouth. Fay's mouth dropped open.

"That's amazing!" She ran over to Buddy and hugged him. "Officer C, let me introduce you to Bella, my new dragon companion!" She whistled and a three-foot dragon flew to us and landed right next to Buddy, who jumped and then sniffed her butt. Bella hissed at Buddy in response.

"Sorry, Buddy, she's still learning her manners!" Fay laughed. She hooked a bungee cord to her waist to propel herself to the ceiling while the dragon flew around the room, so she could essentially fly with the dragon. I was glad to see the fear caused by the events of earlier was fading.

"Don't forget your helmet, Fay," I yelled as I quickly grabbed it from the bleachers. Since this was a boarding school, most of the kids looked at me as a father figure. I was in charge of their physical safety, but the emotional side of things was always hard for me. That's where Buddy came in. He's like an emotional support animal to a lot of the students here; and for me as well.

SWOOSH! Professor Winnow stepped out of another portal on the other side of the room, followed by about 10 students running through. "Sorry, Chinnagen, we've got more for ya!"

I smiled as I saw the kids, ranging from ages 6 to 10, chanting various spells at their personal dragons and running around the room to keep up with them. As I was supervising the bungee flying, one of the students was fidgeting with their harness and looking quite terrified. "Janue, are you okay up there?" I shouted.

Before I could get to the boy, several devious students cast the *wrong spells.* I saw missiles materialize on the ground around me and shoot toward the ceiling. When they exploded, multiple kids came tumbling down, along with pieces of the stone walls around us. I felt my face go pale at the thought of the aftermath.

I ran with Buddy to the outskirts of the room and, by instinct, ducked my head and braced myself to hear the impact of the stone and bodies hitting the floor. When I looked up through the smoke, I realized I'd let go of Buddy's leash and he was sniffing for kids buried under the rubble. I ran to remove stone off multiple bodies, but the stone turned to foam and the floor was pliable and bouncy, like a trampoline.

This room magically transforms in the event of an explosion to protect the students, I remembered Professor Winnow informing me. Not one of the students was harmed. They were just stunned–which explained why they had lain still until Buddy came up and practically licked their faces off.

Though I've only been working for Spellstruck for two years and this was the first time I'd experienced this room transforming, I was a police officer in the magic-less society for ten years. I'd seen some pretty gruesome sights, some that still haunt me to this day. I was feeling really grateful to be at Spellstruck right now. I had found out about the academy through my aunt, whose husband and child were both born with magical abilities and recruited by the school.

Before I knew it, the students were up and bungeeing about again like nothing happened. Just then, I heard Professor Winnow radioing for me.

"Officer Chinnagen, Cal's parents are at the front office wait-ing to see you."

"Acknowledged. I'll be right there."

I quickly radioed Chief Rino, Attorney Jen and our school psychologist and asked them to join me in the conference room.

"Thank you all for meeting with me on such short notice," I said. "As you're aware, we had a very serious incident today with Cal. I found a loaded gun in his backpack. He said he merely wanted to show it to his classmate, who he allegedly got into an argument with and hit yesterday. He is currently being looked over by staff at our hospital to determine if there are any concerns regarding his mental health. I've included Dr. Noble in this meeting to discuss with us what we've learned so far."

"Thank you, Officer Chinnagen," Dr. Noble said. "I am the school psychologist and am assisting staff at our hospital wing with getting Cal the support he needs. Mr. and Mrs. Bartley, we need your consent to begin the evaluation process for an official diagnosis, but we do see signs and symptoms of an Emotional Disturbance in Cal. Have you noticed him having a difficult time getting along with peers his age?"

"We have never noticed any problems at home," Mrs. Bartley said. "He does like to keep to himself, and he can get angry sometimes, but it is usually resolved quickly when we give him some candy or a game to play."

"I see," Dr. Noble said. "I've interviewed several professors who have noted Cal has difficulty expressing himself with them, as well as his peers here at the academy. I've brought the paperwork here to sign for us to proceed with evaluating Cal. We do need these papers to be signed if you wish for Cal to continue at Spellstruck Academy."

"I do not want my son to have an official diagnosis, but I don't see another choice," Mrs. Bartley said.

"We will sign," Mr. Bartley said. "We want Cal to get what he needs. And Spellstruck is the only magical academy in our area. Thank you for working with us to make this right."

"Now, we do need to address the circumstances surrounding Cal's possession of a loaded gun," Attorney Jen began. "Of course, due to Cal's age and possible condition, he will not be charged with any criminal offenses. However, Officer Chinnagen needs to ask you some questions."

"Indeed," I said. "Cal told me he got the gun off the dresser in your room, Mrs. Bartley."

"I keep my gun on the dresser in case of an intrusion; we do not live in a safe area," Mrs. Bartley said.

"Are you aware failing to properly secure your loaded weapon could indicate you are endangering your child and could be a criminal offense?" I asked.

"We did not think of this," Mr. Bartley said.

"I want an attorney," Mrs. Bartley said.

"You definitely have the right to an attorney, and I can contact the court to have one appointed. Since you're requesting an attorney, can I assume you're invoking the rest of your rights at this time and no longer wish to answer any additional questions?" I asked. I hadn't read Mr. or Mrs. Bartley their rights before I started as they weren't technically under arrest and could have left at any time if they decided to. But, now that Mrs. Bartley was asking for an attorney, I figured it was best to assume she, at least, was invoking. If this proceeded to a criminal trial I didn't want to risk losing it over a mistake I made.

"Excuse me officer," Mr. Bartley said. "I think we can deal with this without an attorney."

Mrs. Bartley turned to look at her husband. "Excuse me?"

"What are you suggesting?" I asked.

"Can I assume the weapon you took off my son was destroyed?"

"It was."

"As my wife said, we don't live in a safe neighborhood and do wish to have a gun for protection. However, perhaps you can assist with setting up proper storage for a weapon so Cal can't access it, but it is accessible quickly if needed. The weapon wasn't left out intentionally, and we keep it in order to have a tool to help us protect ourselves and Cal from the dangers we face in our neighborhood."

I glanced at Attorney Jen who nodded. "I would also recommend some home visits by Dr. Noble and Officer Chinnagen to follow up with Cal during the summer. Since Cal will be here for the remainder of the school year, we can limit his visits home until we have been assured any weapons in the house are being properly stored and Cal is being properly supervised."

"Wait," Mrs. Bartley said. "Cal won't be able to come home on weekends?"

"Not until we are sure he will be properly supervised and that any weapons in the home are properly stored and safe," I said.

Mr. Bartley placed a hand on his wife's arm. "This is for the best and you know it."

Buddy walked over and placed his head on Mrs. Bartley's lap, and she started scratching his ears.

Attorney Jen glanced at me. "I'll contact the court. No charges have been made yet. As the Bartley's are allowing us to do the evaluation and treatment for Cal; and since they are requesting to have you assist with safe weapon storage and I would request a firearm's safety class for them both; I believe it's possible the D.A. will agree to diversion."

"Diversion?" Mr. Bartley asked. "Isn't that something that's offered to kids?"

"Normally, yes," Attorney Jen said. "However, it is available to adults as well. What it will mean is that you will both be charged with Reckless Endangerment of a Child. However, if you complete the firearms safety class, perform community service, hours and type of service to be determined by the D.A.'s office, and demonstrate you are creating a safe environment for Cal in your home during the home visits, then the charges will be dismissed and the case sealed."

Mr. Bartley looked at Mrs. Bartley and waited. Buddy raised his head and whined softly as he placed a paw on her hand.

"You're right, this is for the best," she said.

I nodded and smiled at Buddy when he glanced back at me. Yes, this would work out for the best and I would definitely be visiting the Bartley house—not only to help them comply with the conditions of the diversion, but also to take a closer look at the neighborhood they were living in and what steps could be taken to help them feel safer in their home.

The rest of the day passed by quickly after that. Professor Glangow packed up some extra food for our dinner as a thank-you for Buddy's extra-heroic service today. The other thing that happened was that Professor Shadow confirmed the directors of Spellstruck Academy had approved giving Buddy a special enchantment —one that would allow him to age very slowly so he would be able to perform his duties as the K9 of Spellstruck Academy for as long as he and I were willing to do so.

Soon Winnow was opening the portal to send us home and our self-driving car parked itself in our driveway as I led Buddy through the front door. He ran all his energy out in the backyard while I popped open an ice-cold beer and settled onto the couch, feeling grateful for another productive day serving our community.

Buddy fell asleep next to me on the couch after chowing down on more leftover beef, and we were so content to just be together, we didn't even move to our bed that night.

~ * ~ * ~

Kendra grew up in Florida and was introduced to Disney World at a young age. Her interest in the fantasy genre began with a love for fairytales.

Although she wrote nonfiction for a while as a journalist, her desire to write fiction came from her love for fantasy series. She loved reading the Chronicles of Narnia and the Lunar Chronicles as a child, and her husband has recently introduced her to the Stormlight Archive.

In addition to her writing, she has worked as a copy editor at two publication companies, and currently is a middle school drama teacher.

Where the Hearth Is

Lisa Timpf

AI-enhanced border collie Pepper twitched her nose, keeping her eyes tightly closed as she processed her thoughts. That dream she'd just had, of their mission on Altimus—it had seemed so vivid. Right down to the scent of the pine trees that dotted the forest they'd trudged through, enroute to the Syndicate headquarters, the rasp of sedgegrass against her muzzle as they skulked through the meadow.

Wait. That didn't feel like sedgegrass. And it's still there...

Though she'd been retired from the Galactic Space Services for three months, years of rigorous training enabled Pepper to transition instantly into a state of full wakefulness. She scrambled to her feet and shuffled backwards, noticing, as she did so, a black form twitching erratically in the air just above where she'd been sleeping.

On closer examination, the form proved to have eight legs that spanned an area as broad as her dinner bowl.

Spider! Pepper bared her teeth in a snarl. She cocked her head and lowered her lips back over her teeth as logic kicked in. *Spiders aren't native to Arcadia*, she thought. Of course, one could have come in via the spaceport...

...But there were so many checks and balances to prevent that! No, a simpler explanation lurked somewhere near. She felt certain of it.

Pepper ducked her head. Her irrational fear of arachnids had been a source of embarrassment throughout her career as a canine operative in the GSS, though most of her ship-mates had been kind enough not to tease her about it. Most, but not all. And one of those who had derived immense pleasure from leveraging her fear for his own entertainment happened to live with Pepper and her handler Minna, now that they'd moved planet-side.

"Quicksilver!" Pepper yelped.

A handsome silver-grey feline poked his head through the branches of the pine tree Minna and her partner Allie had erected in the home's living room. The cat yanked the string on which the fake spider was suspended one more time for effect, and grinned.

"Very funny," Pepper remarked, making sure her tone conveyed, clearly, her complete lack of amusement. "You'd better not let Minna catch you in there."

"She won't." The cat's voice oozed with self-confidence.

"How can you be so sure?"

Quicksilver clambered down, then picked his way carefully around the brightly wrapped packages arranged at the base of the tree. "Because. I heard her leave in the car. And I'll hear it come back."

Pepper turned away. *She* hadn't heard the vehicle depart. She'd been too deep in sleep. Was she going soft, now that they'd moved dirtside?

"Look, I'm sorry."

Pepper whirled back to face the cat. *It's not like him to apologize.*

"You've seemed down in the mouth lately. I was just trying to cheer you up."

Pepper chuffed softly to herself.

"Is there a problem?" The cat took a step closer.

Nothing I'd tell you, Pepper thought. She believed her reticence to be justifiable, having been the butt of Quicksilver's practical jokes all too often in the three-plus years since she'd first made his acquaintance. Still, with Minna out and Allie having left this morning for Mailletville, two hours' travel each way, the cat presented the only confidante available to her at the moment.

Pepper shuffled her forepaws, uncertain what to do. She shifted position so she could see out the window. See the yellow sky. She still hadn't gotten used to that. Oh, sure, they'd gone on-planet on assignments, back when she, Quicksilver, and Minna had been active GSS operatives. But always, in between, they'd returned to the *Meech Lake*, their vessel. To Minna's comfortable bunk room. To the exercise area. To the mini-caf, where one of the crew members could often be prevailed upon to dial up a dog cookie from the synth-server…

"Do you know what they're doing on the *Meech Lake* right now?" Pepper asked, her voice thick with emotion.

"Barrelling off on some mission to risk life and limb?" Quicksilver sat facing Pepper and curled his tail around his front toes.

Pepper shot the cat a disdainful look. "Getting ready for Christmas."

Though Nibo Salvar, their commanding officer, had been Harsovian, she'd made a point of honouring the winter festivals celebrated by various planetary cultures, including Earth's Christmas. Pepper closed her eyes, remembering the fun of accompanying Minna on her Secret Santa expeditions through the hallways. The smell of special meals programmed into the auto-servers—meals which Minna had often shared with her. The fun of opening gifts, the day of, in Minna's cabin.

"The smell of pine, pumped through the air vents," Pepper said dreamily.

"Are you daft? That was synth-smell. You've got the real thing right in front of you." Quicksilver jerked his head toward the tree.

Pepper ignored the comment. "The carols."

"You can't carry a tune in a bucket." Quicksilver smirked. "I, on the other hand—"

"You call that caterwauling singing?"

"Insults will get you nowhere." Despite the remark, the cat fired Pepper an approving glance. She'd always encouraged her canine counterpart to show more spunk. Trading verbal barbs was something the cat would happily do 24-7. Or, in Arcadia's case, 25-8.

But not Pepper. She yearned for action. "What're you planning for today?"

Quicksilver stretched and yawned. "Well, if there was a blaze going in the fireplace, I'd curl up on the hearth. But instead I think I'll just head over to the master bedroom for a nap."

"Don't you ever get tired of sleeping?"

Quicksilver shot the dog a green-eyed glare. "I have *years* of sleep to catch up on from the *Meech Lake*. And I'd best get started."

Tail in the air, the cat headed for the back bedroom. Pepper snorted in disgust.

Maybe when Minna got home, she could be prevailed on to go for a walk or engage in a rousing game of fetch. Something to look forward to.

Pepper's spirits rose, then just as quickly plummeted.

Who knew when Minna would be home? And lately, she'd seemed too busy to pay much attention to Pepper. Why would today be any different?

A spark of defiance deep within the dog's black and white head flared into a small flame.

Yes, it had been Pepper's own decision to retire. But that didn't make it any easier to accept that life was different now. Harder, in a way, knowing it was her choice. That she feared, deep down, she might have made the *wrong* choice. Perhaps it would have been better to go out in a blaze of glory instead of sitting around the house all day…

Suddenly restless, Pepper slipped through the dog door before she could change her mind.

Once outside, Pepper hesitated. Did a nap sound like such a bad idea? Not necessarily…

She shot a longing glance back at the house and snarled under her breath. If she returned, Quicksilver would never let her hear the end of it.

The breeze ruffled Pepper's fur and tickled her snout. The dog lifted her head, cataloguing the scents. Nothing threatening, nothing surprising. But that, there—

The tang of fish-smell and kelpweed. Which reminded her. Living planet-side might not be as exciting or purposeful as her service on the *Meech Lake*, but they *had* made some friends in the three months they'd lived on Arcadia. And the smell of the large ocean upon whose shores New Caraquet had been built jogged the dog's memory.

Rimbaut Salvage, a business owned by some of those new friends, was a brisk ten-minute trot from her home. Well, eleven minutes, the last time she'd made the trip. *I've let myself get out of shape.* The thought failed to dampen Pepper's spirits, now that she had a goal to shoot for.

Her emotions ratcheted up another notch when she slipped through the salvage operation's open gateway and spotted Anna Rimbaut. The woman, who worked with her three brothers and her father Lazare at the firm, had started keeping dog cookies and cat treats in her desk since befriending Pepper and Quicksilver.

Licking her lips in anticipation, Pepper trotted up to Anna, who stood, tablet in hand, studying one of the vessels the crew had brought in.

Anna lowered the tablet and smiled when spotted the dog. "I was just about to have my tea break," Anna said. "C'mon in."

Obedient to a fault, particularly when it suited her, Pepper trailed the woman through the door of her office, then plopped her behind on the floor and watched, gaze riveted on Anna's right hand as the woman slowly opened the top drawer of the desk.

"Is Minna with you?" Anna asked, tilting her head so she could see back through the corridor.

Pepper woofed twice and shook her head.

Anna laughed. "You do understand a lot, don't you?"

Pepper rose to her feet, wagged her tail, and extended her snout to accept the cookie that Anna held out. She munched on the treat as Anna busied herself with heating the kettle she kept on top of her filing cabinet.

"You know," Anna said. "Dad's just getting the boat ready to go check out a potential salvage site. You'd be welcome to come along. I could check with Minna—"

Pepper raised her head and gazed intently at Anna. A ship— she felt a surge of enthusiasm that quickly ebbed away. The notion of activity appealed, but the realization that the *Northumberland* wasn't the type of ship she yearned to feel under her paws weighed down upon her.

Pepper nodded toward the cookie drawer and woofed softly, a gesture she hoped Anna would interpret as a thank you. Then she squared herself in the direction of the door, looking back over her shoulder at Anna.

"I get it," Anna said, laughing. "You have business of your own to attend to. Another time, perhaps."

Another time. Pepper dipped her muzzle in acknowledgement, then jogged through the door, her pace quickening as she proceeded. Anna's suggestion of taking a trip had brought to mind a different destination. One she knew that Quicksilver would mock her for, if he knew of it.

He won't know of it, Pepper thought. She gritted her teeth.

The spaceport sat on the far edge of town, beyond a low hill that provided ample separation from the residential and business areas. As she approached, Pepper could detect the sweetish smell of the plant-based fuels that powered the servicing trucks and luggage trains.

There. Pepper, having crested the hill, looked down at the spaceport and sighed. She hadn't realized how sore her eyes had been for such a sight. She squinted as sunlight bounced off a shuttle from a passenger liner. A swirl of colour surrounded the vessel as brightly-clad tourists disembarked. Noting the daypacks and the binoculars many sported, Pepper surmised they'd be headed to the Arcadia outback, hoping for a glimpse of the local fauna—the chienchats or the cerfelan or perhaps some of the brilliantly-feathered birds that abounded in Arcadia's woodlands.

Beyond the shuttle, spaceport staff collected a delivery smart-pod that'd been dropped from a transport freighter to parachute down, making auto-corrections with tiny nav-jets to position itself for landing. Two other smartpods squatted on the spaceport tarmac, waiting for their turn to be processed.

Pepper knew the pods emptied on the previous visit had already been reloaded with Arcadian exports, then shot into space to rejoin their parent vessel before it departed for its next stop. She cocked her head and studied the pods, wondering whether they held any goods that Minna might have ordered. Or, for that matter, the special shipment she'd requested…

I should have done this sooner. The bustle of the spaceport, the mere affirmation their quiet planet was linked in some way to the busy commerce of the galaxy, had already lifted her spirits. Pepper glanced at the remaining ships. Two J-class cruisers, the kind favoured by many for sabbatical space-jumps with extended family, sat fins-down further out on the spaceport's surface, and three other vessels rested further toward the periphery.

Pepper's eyes narrowed as she studied the most distant of those, seeing the charred nosecone, the distinctive outline. *It couldn't be. Surely Port Authority would have recognized it…*

But how would they? They weren't the ones who'd run across a vessel very much like this one back on Altimus. Pepper narrowed her eyes, studying the distant shape. If she was right, the vessel was a derelict salvaged from a long-abandoned Greenoan spaceport and rendered space-worthy once again. Only someone desperate would stoop to such measures.

Someone who operated on the fringes of the law, for example.

They'd run across Syndicate operatives in three vessels almost identical to this one, fast-moving smugglers. And captured two of them. But the third had escaped, much to Commander Salvar's chagrin.

And now, it looked as though the fugitive vessel had made landfall here.

The ship sat apart from its fellows, its nose pointed skyward, its sharply angled fins suggesting a readiness for flight. Pepper tilted her head and tried to remember the landing schedule. It was impossible, where they lived, not to hear the growl of incoming jets. She'd thought she detected a rumbling in the night, just after moon high. Against regulations, but then again, what did Syndicate members care for such niceties?

The night-time landing argued for a short visit, a quick turnaround. Here to do their business and then gone before anyone could raise alarm.

If only she could contact Minna!

Not wanting to be tracked, Pepper hadn't brought her com. She raised her lips in a grimace. *I didn't think I'd need it. I'll know better next time.*

Should she contact Xavier Thibodeau of the Arcadian Defense Team? That'd be her next stop. But it was one thing to share a half-baked theory with Minna. Quite another to alert the Defense Team commander about a peril that might or might not be real…

Pepper trotted back down the hill, moving at an angle. Her motions infused with purpose, now, she loped around the berm that circled the spaceport, skirting the scrubland. Noting a tall buroak she'd marked from her original position, she nodded to herself. *Should be able to get a good sightline from here.*

She trotted up the berm, moving with purpose, hanging her tongue out to the side. To a casual observer, she hoped to convey the image of a family dog on the lam.

Her eyes intent, she crept to the crest of the berm, then looked down, feeling a flush of satisfaction. She'd been right, this location provided an excellent vantage point. And there was no mistaking the vessel. The scarring along the sides, the barely-legible markings that had once been Greenoan lettering—it was the same ship they'd encountered on Altimus.

And she was certain it was up to no good.

Now to alert Xavier, before these ones took off.

Pepper had meant to leave immediately. But her yearning for what she had lost, what she had left behind, froze her in her tracks when she heard the rumble of a departing jet.

On the opposite end of the field, flames shot down from below the fins of one of the family cruisers. Ah, to be off for adventures in the skies! She wondered where they might be headed. From here? Maybe Tosorontia, out in the next system. Or Space Station Three, which boasted the galaxy-renowned shopping and clearance centre offering the goods from Karspan Sector. Minna had bought her a blanket there, made of the softest naava spider silk. She still remembered how soft it had felt...

Pepper watched the skybound vessel until it disappeared into the sky. Then she shook herself. She had places to go.

She was about to turn and lope toward town when she heard the scuff of space-boots behind her.

"Well, lookie here."

She didn't recognize the voice, but there was no mistaking the undertone of menace. The fur along Pepper's back bristled.

She turned, slowly, muscles tensing as she readied herself for flight.

Most Arcadians knew her, and she knew them. But the scent of this one was different. He'd been in the outback, she could detect that much. Underlying that was the smell of the space traveller— recirculated air, body smell. Water was at a premium on most ships, but some accommodation was made for periodic bathing. Still, for many spacers, a trip planet-side meant a chance to visit the showers for a real clean-up. This one had not taken that opportunity. Which argued for being on business. In, and out.

Grey form-fitting slacks and tunic, with no insignia. And the weapons slung at his belt—he couldn't have gone to town, not carrying the disruption blaster that hung at his right side. Banned in all sectors. Favoured by outlaws.

A poorly healed scar from an old wound had lain a lash across his cheek. Pepper whimpered low in her throat. She'd seen such, only once, aboard the *Meech Lake*. Knew how long it had taken the bearer of that scar to recover.

Feeling a surge of empathy, she met his gaze. And shivered, seized by a sudden chill. She'd never seen eyes so cold.

Pepper drew to mind the skit nights aboard the *Meech Lake*, entertainments to while away the long hours. Minna had worked patiently with Pepper and Quicksilver, laughingly coaching them in the finer points of play-acting. Time to apply those teachings now.

She nodded politely and turned to go down the hill. *Just a dog out for a walk*, she told herself. *Pretend to be that with all your might.*

She took one step, then another.

"Not so fast."

Pepper turned back to look at the man, her gaze dropping to the blaster he now held in his right hand. Despite her determination to play the role of a carefree family pet, at the sight of the weapon her tail slipped between her legs.

This evoked a sly grin from the spacer. "Hmmm. Now how would an ordinary mutt on Arcadia know what a disruption blaster looks like?"

Pepper offered a slow wag, then cocked her head and studied the man with the most vacant look she could muster. She saw doubt flit across his face and allowed herself to nurse a small spark of hope.

The man glanced at his wrist chrono, then back at the dog. "Gotta make tracks," he said. "Liftoff's in two hours, and it wouldn't do to be left behind." The sincerity with which those words were spoken resonated with Pepper. He meant every word. "And whether you're smart or not, you're coming with me. There's a market for your sort, out there."

Pepper bared her teeth. Fight, or flight? Despite the threat implicit in the weapon, would he destroy a potential source of income?

She knew the answer to that. If it came down to dealing with to a potential threat to the ship, he'd do far worse. Besides, the less lethal paralyzer slung on the other hip would provide a way to deal with her without killing her.

Pepper paddled her forepaws on the ground, expressing a genuine distress.

"Ahead of me. Nice and easy. And don't try any funny stuff." The man bared his own teeth in a grin.

What was it Commander Salvar always said? As she stumbled along ahead of the Syndicate man, Pepper clung to the memory of her former boss as an island of sanity in what had become an upside-down world. Stay in the game, that's what she'd said. Stay in the game; and look for your chances.

Pepper darted a glance at the vessels drawing ever nearer. Was it just this morning that she'd longed to go back into space?

Be careful what you wish for. That was another saying Commander Salvar had been particularly fond of.

She wished she'd paid greater heed.

Pepper slowed her pace as the Syndicate vessel drew closer, scuffing her feet.

Should she run for it, in spite of everything? She glanced ahead.

Nothing even faintly resembling cover, to hide behind. He'd have a clear shot, and unless he had an abysmally poor aim—

Pepper cut the thought off right there. Syndicate operatives with lousy aims didn't typically survive for long. And this one's facial scarring and arrogant air argued he'd been around for awhile. No, she'd have to come up with a different plan.

Where there's life, there's hope. That thought had sustained her through difficult situations before.

But as the ship's entry-ramp loomed closer, Pepper's thoughts turned to Minna, and to the possibility that once the ship blasted, she might never see her handler again. Despite all of her training, despite all of the difficult situations she'd been through, she couldn't help it.

She raised her head and gave tongue to her despair in a long and wavering howl.

Pepper awoke with a stun-inspired headache. *Not the first time,* she told herself, raising her head and regretting that too-quick movement immediately.

She had the sense that some sound had woken her. If so, it had since faded from earshot.

Pepper raised her head. Despite a wave of dizziness, she forced herself to focus. Time was short, and she couldn't afford to waste it. Giving voice to the howl of despair must have triggered her captor to hit her with the paralyzer. Which meant she'd been out for thirty minutes to an hour, depending on the duration of the raying.

Pepper closed her eyes and focussed on what her nose could

tell her. The distinctive smell of ship-air, cut with disinfectant. Whoever had done the cleaning hadn't been super-thorough. Bio-smell of body oils and skin flakes could still be detected, albeit faintly.

There. The scent of haava smoke. Pepper coughed. Marcat spice, too, tickled her nose, telling her the vessel had among its crew a Galvan. Then again, if one of the eye-stalked natives of Galva paced the corridors on a ship like this, she couldn't count on their normal reputation for empathy for all living things. That would have been distorted, somehow, for him to serve on a ship such as this one.

The dog opened her eyes and began a visual examination of her accommodation. Metal surrounded her, too close on all sides. She had barely enough room to turn around. The thick criss-crossed wire of the enclosure's door offered the only large opening, though a fine meshwork in the back of the pen offered a flow of air. At least there was an auto-fill water bowl, with the usual taste of recirc water replaced by the clean spring-fed Arcadian liquid. So, they'd taken time while portside to refresh their supplies. Which could be a bad thing, Pepper thought. It could signal their intent to make a long jump back into space.

One thing at a time.

Voices, just outside the door to the room in which she'd been penned, alerted her to danger. Striving to present an image that might look, for all the world, as though she still slept Pepper curled into a ball, covering her nose with her tail. If she was lucky, her captor would believe the stun-shot still held its effect.

The door slid open with a hiss.

"You were freelancing." Words spoken in an accusatory tone, by a voice she didn't recognize.

Pepper inhaled deeply, detecting the scent-signatures of two individuals—her captor, and another.

"Providence sent her," Pepper's captor grunted. "She'll fetch a good price at Beta Station."

Pepper's spirits sank. *Beta Station.* Reputed to be the Syndicate stronghold, though no-one was certain of its location. If she'd worn her homing device, she might lead the GSS to its location…

But she wasn't GSS anymore, was she? And who would come to look for her? She hadn't told Minna where she was going,

Quicksilver either. For all they knew, she might be out on the waves with the Rimbauts, or exploring the outback looking to make contact with the elusive chienchats.

"Well cared for, by someone," the newcomer said. "Greater odds somebody will come looking."

"We lift in an hour," Pepper's captor replied. "No time. They wouldn't have even noticed she was missing. And the fact she's in good shape will mean she'll draw a better price."

"If Harfor finds out what you've done…"

"When does he ever come down to the cargo area?" A pause, then the Syndicate man answered his own question. "Never. We're safe here."

"I'll keep my silence. But there'll be a price."

"Isn't there always?"

The voices moved away, and Pepper rose to her feet, stretching to relieve a kink in her right haunch. *An hour,* she thought. *That's not much time.*

In that case, she'd better get busy.

Every instinct urged Pepper to batter herself against the door of her cage. To dig at her housing, hoping to find a weak point, until her paws bled.

But she forced herself to slow down. To use the superior intelligence the AI implant afforded her.

Best start with the door-latch.

The door wouldn't have been designed to open from the inside. But then again, it was meant to keep ordinary animals penned. And she was not an ordinary animal…

Pepper studied the door's opening mechanism with care. When her examination was concluded, she breathed a sigh of relief. Such had been made to keep in non-sentient beasts, and would, she was certain, do an admirable job of that. But for an AI-enhanced entity such as her, mastering the lock would be possible. Move her unusually agile front toes so, and so; support the catch mechanism with her muzzle, thus—the door popped open.

Pepper stood framed in the opening, triangular ears pricked at their highest to catch any scintilla of sound. Then she pushed the door open and hopped out onto the floor.

Now, to find the entry-door to this cramped tin can. Driven by urgency, she padded down the narrow corridor, all senses on high alert.

Look for high traffic. And follow the trail back...

There, she'd done it. The entryway stood before her. And with it, her hope of reunion with Minna...

She was in luck. No Syndicate operatives in sight, though surely they'd have set an alarm to alert them to the presence of anyone breaching the perimeter defense without the access code.

So, she'd set off the alarm when she went through that. But if she was lucky, if she ran quickly enough, there'd be a chance...

About to leap through the opening, Pepper heard a commotion above her, toward the passenger decks.

Nothing to do with me, she thought.

Then she heard Minna's voice.

Mastering ship-stairs had been one of the toughest tasks in Pepper's GSS training. The border collie appreciated the skill now, clambering, despite the lack of mag-boots, with an agility born of long practice and heat-of-the-moment urgency.

As she scaled the steps, her mind churned. What was Minna doing here? Had her foolishness drawn her master into peril?

Pepper whimpered to herself as she ascended the final rung and popped out onto the next floor.

To her relief, she spotted Minna's tall, slim form in the corridor that led to the right.

"All clear," a helmet-and-armor clad Port Authority officer told Minna. He paused. "But no sign of..." His eyes widened as he spotted Pepper.

Minna, curious as to what had caused his sudden silence, turned to look. She dropped on one knee and seized Pepper's head between her hands. "There you are. I was so worried."

"Worried?" The Port Authority agent raised his eyebrows. "You mean, you didn't send her here on surveillance?"

"No." The response was short, sharp, and emphatic. Minna rose to her feet, her expression grim. "In fact, I just happened to be at the customs office picking up a parcel when I thought I *heard* her. If it hadn't been for that..."

"Excuse me a moment." The officer turned away, right hand pressed to his ear, then turned back. "Well, either way, her presence proved fortuitous. Gave us grounds for a search. And we found a large quantity of snort and other contraband. So, this ship won't be lifting any time soon."

"Good," Minna said.

The officer put his hand to his ear again, then said, "Something I need to check on. You're okay to see yourself out?"

"Yes, and thank you."

The officer departed, and Minna turned her full attention to Pepper. "We," she said, her voice low, "are going to talk. At home. Unless you'd rather stay shipboard?" She shot the dog a keen look.

Pepper shook her head. Home it was.

The dog turned toward the stairs, then shot a yearning look back at her master. That backward glance proved fortuitous.

Because just behind Minna, she saw the wall moving, where the wall shouldn't be able to move.

A hidden compartment, Pepper told herself. Of course. Such a ship would be full of those...

She jerked her head toward the threat, then leaped.

And realized how out of practice she was.

Her shoulder slammed against the now-visible door in the wall, and she fell to the ground with a grunt of pain. She should have waited, timed her jump differently...

The door flew open. Minna stood, gun drawn, face grim. Pepper staggered to her feet. *I'll be too late,* she thought, bracing herself for a leap.

And she might have been, had the young man hiding behind the panel been carrying a weapon.

But he was not.

This was no hardened criminal. A nav-man, or perhaps a tube-jockey, working an apprenticeship down in the ship's power plant. He'd simply sought refuge the first place he could think of. And elected to show himself too soon.

Lucky for us, Pepper thought.

She exchanged a look with Minna, tail tucked.

Though the start was less than auspicious, the promised talk when Minna and Pepper got home wasn't as bad as it could have been.

They'd waited till Quicksilver was out of the room. Then Minna had sat on the couch, Pepper seated in front of her on the floor.

"Look, you shouldn't have taken off like that."

I know. I know. Pepper lowered her head. *I'm not sure what got into me. Well, I am. But it shouldn't have. I wish it hadn't.*

As though sensing her troubled thoughts, Minna had reached down to rub Pepper's ears, just the way the border collie liked.

"You know, don't you, that it was the right time to retire?" Minna asked.

Pepper whimpered softly.

"I miss them, too. But we can't jump back into the past," Minna. "We need to live in the present. Find a purpose here. It's an adjustment for all of us."

Pepper tilted her head. She hadn't considered that others might share the same feeling.

"Look, it's been crazy busy since we got here. There's been a lot for us to do, to get organized. I don't expect you to understand."

Pepper looked up at Minna, seeing the doubt in her eyes. The yearning to be understood.

I'll try. Pepper rested her Minna's knee.

"There is—something. But I don't want to get your hopes up." Minna bit her lower lip, then shook her head. "Not yet." She paused. "Want to go for a walk?"

Is the sky blue? Er, I mean yellow? Can we? Can we?

"I'll take that as a yes."

Sensing she'd been forgiven, Pepper wagged her tail.

Two weeks later, Pepper felt only contentment as she sprawled on the rug at Minna's feet. She raised her head, looked around the living room, and opened her jaws in a grin. Anyone entering the house without understanding the context might have thought the place had been invaded by plimrats, the gopher-like creatures in Arcadia's outback that loved to steal and hoard anything they could get their dextrous paws on.

What do you expect, on Christmas Day, Pepper thought. Quicksilver, lying on his side, batted lazily at the box of hardplas spiders she'd bought him. When he'd opened the gift, he'd shot her a quizzical glance. She'd shrugged and told him the current lot were getting tatty. If he wanted her fright to be real, he'd best up his game.

So you like it, being scared, he'd asked her.

She'd just given him an inscrutable border collie look. Let him think what he wanted.

"So, Pepper, d'you like it?" Minna held up the locally-fabbed flak jacket she and Allie had given the border collie as a gift.

Pepper tapped her tail against the floor twice to signal her approval. Then a thought hit her. *When will I get to use it?*

Did it really matter? She'd realized, back on the Syndicate ship, retirement was a reality she had to face, not a situation she needed to run from. She'd just have to learn to cope, that's all.

Allie cleared her throat. "That leaves one last—gift, I think." She raised her eyebrows and looked at Pepper and Quicksilver in turn. "Not the kind you wrap."

Quicksilver laid back his ears. "If you couldn't wrap it, then it's not something you can eat, play with, or sleep on," he whispered to Pepper.

Pepper shifted position, unwilling to confront the cat but disagreeing nonetheless. Her new-found acceptance of her lot in life seemed like a gift, in and of itself. If only she could convince Minna that she was okay, now…

Allie cleared her throat. "This's what we've been working toward for the past few months." She exchanged a goofy grin with Minna. "We just had to deal with the red tape, first."

"Tape?" Quicksilver rolled smoothly to his feet. "They should have called on me. I know how to take care of tape, for petesake." He stood on his hind legs and swatted the air to demonstrate.

"Not that kind of tape," Pepper hissed.

"We've got our detective licence. We're cleared to operate on Arcadia, now. Take on cases."

Afterward, Pepper would tell anyone who was willing to listen that she'd tried, really tried, to contain herself. But she couldn't help it. She was on her feet, chasing her tail, before she could stop to think, and did three complete rotations before succumbing to dizziness.

She flopped to the floor, waiting for the mocking comment

that was sure to come from Quicksilver. But the cat, it appeared, had launched himself on a quick circuit of the room, leaping on and off each piece of furniture he encountered, then clambering up the tree for his finale. Right up to the tippy-top.

Said tree was, at the moment, swaying perilously, leaving the cat clinging with all his might, his expression morphing into something resembling seasickness.

Allie walked over to rescue him, and he flowed gracefully onto her shoulders, looking imperiously down at the dog as the tall woman returned to her chair.

"Sorry we didn't tell you earlier," Minna said, after allowing a couple of minutes for everyone to settle down. "We didn't want to get your hopes up if it wasn't going to come to fruition."

So that's what she was talking about. Pepper rose, shook herself, then walked over to Minna and gazed up adoringly. It was the best way she knew how to say, *Everything's going to be okay for sure, now.*

They stayed that way for a long moment, communing silently.

The last of the discontent that had nagged at Pepper two weeks ago ebbed away. Everything she needed was right here. Minna was happy because she was with Allie. Pepper was happy because she was with Minna.

And, of course, there was Quicksilver, too. She'd gotten used to the grey cat, she realized. What if he'd gone off, instead of her?

She'd have missed him, that's what.

"Look," she said, looking up at the cat. "I'm sorry I ran off without saying anything. I—wasn't myself."

The cat stared down at her, his expression inscrutable. For a moment, Pepper thought he was going to play the usual card of unconcern. But instead, he twitched his whiskers and said, "So. You'll be helping us on cases again. That's good news, I suppose."

"Me? Helping you?" Pepper sputtered. "Why, I'll have you know—"

Sensing one of their interminable arguments about to erupt, Minna intervened. "What about a few carols, huh? Like old times."

Pepper, knowing which 'old times' that remark referred to, shot her master a look. Another affirmation that Minna, too, harboured some nostalgia for the old days.

"Wreck the Halls," Quicksilver suggested.

"Bark the Herald Angels Sing!" Pepper yapped.

The cat shot a meaningful look at the box of fake spiders, then at Pepper. "Have a Crawly, Jolly Christmas."

Allie rolled her eyes. "Silent Night it is."

After a spirited round of carol-singing, Pepper curled up on the floor, making sure to lie on Minna's foot so she'd be aware if the woman were to move.

"D'you really think everything's going to be okay with them?" Minna asked Allie. "You know, after—"

Pepper eased an ear backward, the better to take in the conversation.

"It'll be fine. You'll see. It's all still new. But in time, they'll accept this place as home. We all will."

Home, Pepper thought. She yawned. Some days, her memories were vivid. But on other occasions, the adventures they'd had aboard the *Meech Lake* seemed like they'd happened to someone else, the stuff of space-vids.

The dog raised her head, looking around the comfortable room. The handmade rug that provided just the right amount of padding from the floor. The fireplace which, thanks to Allie's efforts earlier that morning, set out an agreeable warmth.

She thought about the close quarters on board the Syndicate ship, and shuddered. She hadn't realized how claustrophobic a vessel could be, once you'd become accustomed to open air. Of course, if Minna chose, she'd follow her right back onto the *Meech Lake* or any other space-faring vessel. But if she had her druthers, she realized she'd be just fine with staying on Arcadia for the rest of her days.

Pepper blinked lazily at Quicksilver, who padded over to touch noses with her.

"Well? Are you home to stay?" The cat studied her with yellow-green eyes. "Not that I care. Although I would hate to waste those excellent spiders. I suppose I could scare Allie with them."

"Scare Allie? That'll be the day."

Quicksilver turned to shoot an appraising look at the woman. "Everyone is afraid of something," he said. "We just haven't found out what."

"Let's hope we don't."

"Well? You haven't answered my question. Do I need to keep an eye on you in case you wander off again?" The cat's whiskers twitched.

"No." Pepper said. She opened her mouth in a grin. "I'm home, now."

"Home," the cat said. He stalked across the room and settled himself comfortably on the tiled flooring in front of the fireplace. "Home is where the hearth is."

Pepper shot him a glare. "*Heart*. It's where the *heart* is."

"Hearth." His voice raised, ever so slightly.

Pepper replied in kind. "Heart."

"Hearth."

"See?" Allie's voice contained a hint of laughter. "Things are pretty much back to normal."

"Not yet," Minna said. She glanced at Pepper, then Quicksilver, mock frowning. "Knock it off, you two," she said.

That's what she used to do on the Meech Lake. *When we got too rowdy.* Instead of experiencing a pang for her former residence, Pepper felt a sense of rightness. Of a cycle, come complete.

Home, Pepper thought, suddenly feeling drowsy. *Home is where Minna is.*

She turned to tell the cat. *Already snoring.*

Would a nap be such a bad idea? She thought not. And the hearth was plenty big enough for both of them…

~ * ~ * ~

Lisa Timpf is a retired HR and communications professional who lives in Simcoe, Ontario, Canada. Her speculative fiction has appeared in a variety of venues, including *New Myths, Future Days, From a Cat's View,* and *Acceptance: Stories at the Centre of Us.* Lisa's speculative haibun collection, *In Days to Come,* is available from Hiraeth Publishing. You can find out more about Lisa's writing at lisatimpf.blogspot.com/.

Mick and Me

Jean Martin

Donnie's, got this tee shirt. It says, "They Don't Pay Me Enough to Do This Job". That's his philosophy of life.

Okay, we don't make what city cops make. Of course we don't have the training city cops get. Bellwood is a small town. Crime here is some asshole driving his ATV down Maple Avenue, or a bunch of kids having a kegger in Brady's Woods.

We got three K9s, Rusty, Sadie and Mick. Mick's the one I take with me when I go to the schools.

Every Fall, me and Mick go to Rhys Elementary and Connors Middle School, to talk to the kids.

I tell the kids at Rhys, to be careful crossing streets, and look out when they get on and off the bus.

I tell the kids at Connors not to use drugs, and to tell a grownup if someone they know has a gun.

Kids at Rhys all watch "Paw Patrol". They like me and Mick. Kids at Connors know TV isn't real. Let's just say they're skeptical, when I tell them the cops are their friends.

With cops like Donnie on the force, I can understand why. That jackass put a ten-year-old in handcuffs once.

The poor kid's asshole friends dared him to say oink oink where Donnie could hear him. Donnie was offended, so he cuffed him, brought him in and wanted to book him, except his parents showed up with a lawyer.

They were going to sue the borough.

Right, it is not okay to say someone is a pig. But kids are dumb. They do dumb things, like taking dares. Being dumb is not a crime. If it was, there would be a lot of politicians behind bars, including most of the Bellwood Borough Council.

We got a call, Friday morning, somebody's got a gun, and he shot the cook and the assistant manager at the Denny's over on 28. The shooter's still out there, driving an old green truck.

His name is Kyle. He's 19. He worked at the Denny's, until last week, when he got into a shouting match with the cook and got fired.

Word gets out, if you see him, don't confront him. He's got a semi-automatic. Wait until the county police and the sheriff's department get here and let them deal with him.

That almost makes sense, until we start getting calls from Rhys Elementary.

Kids are on their phones, calling 911, saying there's a guy with a gun outside their school.

I get a call, go to Courtland Street, and keep people away from the school, but don't do anything. Let the county take care of the shooter. They ain't paying us enough to risk our lives.

So, Mick and me sit in my car, on one end of the street. On the other end, I can see Donnie, sitting in his car with a Big Gulp, a freaking Big Gulp! Like it's a high school football game or something.

Every now and then, I heard gunshots.

I saw the beat up old green truck parked in front of the driveway. I saw the kid, outside the school, pulling at one of the doors.

Then he fired his gun up in the air a few times, to let the kids know he's there.

It's the kind of gun that can kill thirty people in forty seconds.

Mick was going crazy: barking and jumping at the window. He wanted to get out and do his job.

Which was not what I told the folks at city hall.

I told them, I thought Mick needed to water a fire hydrant, so I let him out, and he took off before I could get his leash on him.

Mick knew what to do. He ran straight for the shooter and grabbed his arm.

The kid struggled, but Mick held on, like he was trained to.

Kid tried to shoot Mick and shot himself in the foot. He swore and dropped the gun.

Someplace inside the school, a woman screamed.

Mick held on, until the sheriff's deputy showed up and cuffed the shooter and hauled him off to the ER.

All the kids and the teachers at Rhys elementary went home to their families that night.

They got the day off the next day.

I got reprimanded for ignoring orders, but not where anyone could hear.

Mick was on the news that night, on all the networks, including CNN and MSNBC. He's up for some kind of commendation.

Donnie and his Big Gulp were also on all the networks, including CNN and MSNBC. Everybody knows who he is, that he sat in his car drinking soda pop, while some guy was trying to kill kids. He had to take down all his social media accounts, because he was getting a lot of not so nice messages.

He's leaving the force. He's going into private security. He says it will pay better, and the hours will be easier.

Next week the kids at Rhys Elementary are giving a party for Mick and me. I told them Mick can't have chocolate, 'cause it's bad for dogs. So, they're having a special cake for him, made with cheese and bacon.

Donnie was right, you know. They don't pay us enough to do our jobs. But there are other rewards.

~ * ~ * ~

Jean Martin has a BS degree in Journalism from Ohio University and has been laughing about it for longer than she cares to admit. She lives, at present, in McKeesport, Pennsylvania, with an orange tabby cat named Samwise, who likes bagpipe music.

K9 Jinx

EPSO Deputy Nicholas Witherite

Special thanks to the following:

Hancock family, Sgt. Brad Bengford, EPSO Tactical Support Unit, EPSO Special Response Team, CSPD K9, Fountain Police Department, Manitou Springs Police Department, Greg and Randy Johnson of Johnson K9, Ben Rader of Rader K9, Adam Watson of Phoenix K9, Tom Cordova, John Kay, Animal ER Care, and Faithful Friends Animal Hospital. There are many other VIP's present today, you know who you are and thank you for attending.

So, I wanted this to be a little more relaxed and different than most services we attend during these tragic events. I know Ronnie wanted more smiles than tears so that's why I have props.

Onion—This is significant for a few reasons. First, it's a symbol of what every handler goes through working a police dog. Lots of layers, selection, bond, training, deployments, the ups, downs, the successes, the proud moments, the damn it dog you pooped in the bad guys house again, even after watching you for 10 minutes before releasing you in. Second, it's a scapegoat for when I cry, I'm blaming it on this onion, and you can't judge me.

Shock Collar—We consider this piece of equipment our quarter mile leash. I have one attached to my ankle and a VIP has the remote in their possession to keep me from rambling and talking too long. I would have given it to my wife, but she would use it just to punish me or for pure enjoyment.

By the way I know the pollen and dust are crazy in the building today so if you get teary eyed, we can all blame it on that…

A few days after the incident I was having dinner with Ronnie and Julie and I asked if they wanted to say anything during the ceremony. Julie respectively declined, and Ronnie remained the strong silent type and declined as well. I explained to Ronnie that Brad previously told me he didn't want to speak because he didn't want to be a blubbering fool on stage. Plus, I didn't think the venue even had a speaker system loud enough to hear his voice. (You can put my write-up in my box with the rest of them.)

So then there is me…during this same conversation Ronnie and I talked about how well we clicked as a team, we have super similar thought processes for deployments, training techniques when it came to K9s, cop work in general, family, love for dogs, food (we both loooooove cheesecake). You remember that time I almost gave you and Brad diabetes with my triple chocolate cheesecake? MMmmmm man that was good.

But there is one thing we are complete opposites on… Ronnie like I said before, is the strong silent type, one to keep to himself, no credit type of guy, and me, well I love to talk and will talk to anyone who's willing to listen and sometimes people who are not willing to listen. Now you know why the E-Collar.

I went on and asked what I could do for both Ronnie and Julie. Julie was quick to say, "we need Nick to be Nick." So sorry Sheriff Elder, Julie gave me permission…everybody else strap in and enjoy the ride.

The EPSO K9 Unit was reestablished in 2003. The unit was allotted five K9 teams but was only manned with four dual purpose K9 teams. I transferred to the Unit in late 2017 and Ronnie transferred to the unit in early 2018. Currently EPSO K9 has only two dual purpose teams, we oversee one single purpose K9 assigned to the Rural Outreach Unit, and we have added one single purpose K9 assigned to the Criminal Justice Center.

Since Ronnie and I are the only two dual purpose dog handlers, we have gone through a lot together. We have teammates, mentors, instructors, and leaders within the agency. But most importantly we have become best friends.

It's really easy to only see all the fun things K9 handlers get to do on a daily basis. What better job than to play with dogs on a daily basis? Playing ball, teaching your dog to sit, belly rubs and puppy kisses. Now although those are the best parts, especially belly rubs, this is not all that comes with this job.

El Paso County is roughly twice the size of Rhode Island at 2160 square miles. It is the most populated county in Colorado having almost 750K residents. Having that in mind EPSO dual purpose K9s support a vast number of areas.

Areas supported by us are: EPSO Law Enforcement Bureau, Patrol Division (we're still cops first), EPSO Investigations, EPSO Detention Bureau, EPSO SWAT, EPSO SRT (Special Response Team), every school manned with an SRO (School Resource Officer) provided by EPSO, Colorado State Patrol working within EPSO jurisdiction, DEA, FBI, ATF, Violent Offender Task Force, Metro VNI (Vice, Narcotics Investigations), Fountain Police Department, Fountain Police Department RRT (Rural Response Team), Manitou Springs, Monument Police Department, Calhan Police Department.

EPSO K9 has assisted on military instillations to include, Ft. Carson, Peterson AFB, and the Air Force Academy. We have performed Presidential Details, public demonstrations, and much, much more.

It's easy to think our job is simple, yet no one other than handlers actually know what our job consists of. Supporting these various places can be tough with just the two of us. Stress on our families, missed kids' volleyball and soccer games, taking two vehicles to Thanksgiving dinner at the in laws because there's a chance you will get called out. Being called out in the middle of the night to track a wanted robbery suspect after working a 14-hour shift. Or even getting calls at three in the morning from a local DEA Agent who has info on ten pounds of meth coming up the interstate in a few hours.

Ronnie and Jinx have sacrificed countless numbers of hours honing their skills to be the best team possible. Sleepless nights, multiple missed functions, shortened vacations, long days, and battling extreme weather conditions all without complaint. You must remember while everyone else was cozy in their warm bed, they were the keepers of the night no matter what the situation was.

You may be asking yourself, why would anyone put

themselves through all that? Well Ronnie being as selfless as they come, he does to this to protect his family, his friends, his neighbors, his community and most importantly, ALL citizens and visitors of El Paso County.

The night of April 11, 2022, changed the EPSO K9 unit forever.

Shortly before midnight, my work phone started ringing. I started scrapping the sleepies out of my eyes, whipping the drool off my face and began fumbling around trying to grab my phone. I could see the caller ID was Sgt. Bengford (do not answer). I figured he was calling to tell me of JUST another K9 assist, or JUST another agency assist, or JUST another phone call telling me stop being a bad influence on Ronnie by doing hood rat stuff with my friends that he will have to explain to the commander.

So, as I was debating on even answering his call, since he never calls saying I can have extra days off, or the K9 cameras we have been begging for, for over a year, were finally ordered, or the new unmarked cars we desperately need were given the green light. I realized it was almost midnight and since he is a day shift supervisor, he wasn't just calling to hear my voice.

I answered the call. I could hear pain in his voice. He told me he was going to the vet. I thought it was maybe for one of his personal dogs and he needed help with something. I, for the second time in my life, was very, very wrong.

Brad told me Jinx had been shot and killed on a call earlier in the night. I was speechless. I didn't ask questions. Somehow, I managed to put pants on and make it out the door. I didn't know what I needed to do or where to go, I just knew I needed to see Ronnie.

As I was driving to the Vet, I could hear dispatch still had the channel coded…but no one was saying anything. My mind began racing and I thought the worst thing possible, K9 down, Officer down. There was no information being shared.

I made it to the vet and could see Ronnie's truck parked sideways in a few spots. When I made it inside, I could see Brad standing outside a room at the end of what seemed like the longest hallway ever. (It was actually only three rooms). Once I got to Brad, he just pointed me into the room.

I opened the door and saw Ronnie clutching Jinx and Seth Fritsche covering his face with his hands. I was crushed.

At that moment all I could do was hug Ronnie. I wanted to take all the pain and sorrow away from Ronnie, but I knew I couldn't.

I was later filled in on a few details about the incident which took place. I learned no officers were injured but unfortunately the suspect lost his life. It's no small feat being involved in a situation where someone losses their life.

K9 Handlers are tasked with responding to the worst situations you could possibly imagine and with little to no time to process are forced to make decisions. There is a saying we use often: Paws before boots. We have the mindset to utilize a police K9 in situations where it's too dangerous for humans to go in first; knowing the training we do will provide the safest outcome for everyone involved.

The decision to utilize Jinx as a less than lethal option in that situation, ultimately cost Jinx his life, but Jinx proudly and without hesitation, sacrificed his life to protect his handler, officers on scene, and the community which was in direct line of fire from the suspect.

We could not be more proud of Jinx. He will forever be a hero.

One of my favorite stories about Ronnie and Jinx was during the selection process.

After watching hours of video, looking over x-rays, and researching blood lines, Jinx was selected to become a member of the EPSO family. I remember telling myself if Ronnie didn't want Jinx I sure did. I planned on telling Ronnie the dog was no good for him. My plan was to have him work Taz and I work Jinx…Ronnie didn't fall for my tricks.

Jinx needed to be flown in. I remember getting pictures of Jinx dressed up with "service dog" patches on his harness. The pictures also showed him in a leather agitation muzzle. I thought to myself "what kind of service dog needs a muzzle?" Then I remembered the guy who was bringing him in… He also needed a muzzle, so it worked out just fine.

Once he arrived, I couldn't be there for the delivery to Ronnie. A few days later I met up with Ronnie and started watching their training. After watching for about an hour I realized something. Jinx was WAAAAAY smarter than Ronnie. I mean the dog understood French and well...Ronnie's experience with French is seeing a picture from elementary school of the Eiffel Tower. So the ball was back in my court for trading dogs.

I tried to use the French thing to my advantage. Every time Jinx would crush a scenario, a dope run, a building search, or just grow as a police K9, Ronnie would have to praise him. Now Ronnie would always say "good boy" as he should, but every time I was around him, I would make him say "Oui Oui." Ronnie never fell for my constant clowning of him.

Their bond was like no other I have ever seen. A man and his dog. His furry kangaroo tornado with teeth. His four-legged best friend, and ultimately his savior.

Here's to you Jinx. You are the bestest, most goodest boy. Oui Oui buddy, Oui Oui.

Attention all units.
Please stand by for the last call for K9 Jinx

K9 Jinx from Dispatch...

K9 Jinx from Dispatch...

K9 Jinx from Dispatch...

K9 Jinx you are a true warrior that gave the ultimate
sacrifice and saved the life of others. Your heroic actions
will never be forgotten. Thank You for your bravery and
years of service. You will forever remain in our hearts.
May your days be filled with fetch, all the treats and
endless belly rubs.

Rest easy K9 Jinx we have the watch from here.

End of Watch April 11, 2022

JINX'S LAW
Help change our laws in Colorado for our working K9s

Petition started by Julie Hancock

I'm writing this because this is something I deeply care about and it won't happen without the support of people like you!!! Starting a petition isn't something I would normally do, but I was moved to do so because of what our family went through last year.

My husband is a K9 handler with EPSO, his K9 Jinx was killed in the line of duty on April 11, 2022 in Manitou Springs. He was the 2nd K9 in the state of Colorado to have been killed in the line of duty. Had Jinx's killer lived, he would have only faced felony animal cruelty charges, which would have been nothing more than a slap on the wrist. Because of Jinx's warrior heart and bravery, 4 LEOs went home to their families that night!

I want to ensure our K9s are recognized as sworn officers/deputies and NOT looked at as a piece of equipment. We need harsh punishment for anyone that injures or kills a working K9! Also, when one of our K9s are injured in the line of duty, we need to make sure they receive immediate care with transport by ambulance, as time is critical and this could save their life.

I know I am not alone and together we can make this change happen! PLEASE sign and share!

https://www.change.org/p/jinx-s-law-help-change-our-laws-in-colorado-for-our-working-k9s